# cathy cassidy

# Dizzy

PUFFIN

PUFFIN BOOKS

Published by the Penguin Group
Penguin Books Ltd, 80 Strand, London WC2R ORL, England
Penguin Group (USA) Inc., 375 Hudson Street, New York, New York 10014, USA
Penguin Group (Canada), 90 Eglinton Avenue East, Suite 700, Toronto, Ontario, Canada M4P 2Y3
(a division of Pearson Penguin Canada Inc.)
Penguin Ireland, 25 St Stephen's Green, Dublin 2, Ireland (a division of Penguin Books Ltd)
Penguin Group (Australia), 250 Camberwell Road, Camberwell, Victoria 3124, Australia
(a division of Pearson Australia Group Pty Ltd)
Penguin Books India Pvt Ltd, 11 Community Centre, Panchsheel Park, New Delhi – 110 017, India
Penguin Group (NZ), cnr Airborne and Rosedale Roads, Albany, Auckland 1310, New Zealand
(a division of Pearson New Zealand Ltd)
Penguin Books (South Africa) (Pty) Ltd, 24 Sturdee Avenue, Rosebank, Johannesburg 2196, South Africa

Penguin Books Ltd, Registered Offices: 80 Strand, London WC2R ORL, England

puffinbooks.com

First published 2004
1

This edition published for The Book People Ltd,
Hall Wood Avenue, Haydock, St Helens, WA11 9UL

Copyright © Cathy Cassidy, 2004
All rights reserved

The moral right of the author has been asserted

Set in 13/16.5 pt Monotype Baskerville
Typeset by Rowland Phototypesetting Ltd, Bury St Edmunds, Suffolk

Made and printed in England by Clays Ltd, St Ives plc

British Library Cataloguing in Publication Data
A CIP catalogue record for this book is available from the British Library

ISBN: 978-1-856-13240-4

www.greenpenguin.co.uk

Penguin Books is committed to a sustainable future
for our business, our readers and our planet.
The book in your hands is made from paper
certified by the Forest Stewardship Council.

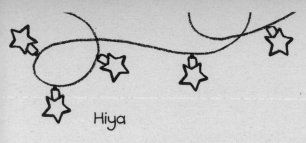

Hiya

I thought I'd tell you a bit about myself. I live in the Scottish countryside with my husband and our two children, a girl and a boy. We also have three cats, two rabbits and a mad, hairy lurcher very like Leggit in this story!

When I'm not writing books I work as an art teacher travelling around the local primary schools, and also as the agony aunt for a magazine. I've always loved daydreaming and inventing stories, and the stories just got bigger and bigger until they had to be told. Some of the ideas in Dizzy come from real life – I used to be a chocolate-eating vegan, and I still drink yukky herb tea! I also have a slightly charred toy mouse stuck to my pinboard, but that's another story . . .

I hope you enjoy reading this as much as I enjoyed writing it.

Best wishes,

Cathy Cassidy

xxxx

cathycassidy.com

*Books by Cathy Cassidy*

# DIZZY
# DRIFTWOOD
# INDIGO BLUE
# SCARLETT
# SUNDAE GIRL
# LUCKY STAR

# Thanks!

To Catriona, who told me to stop daydreaming and start writing – and gave great feedback and advice. To Liam, for putting up with my stressy, can't-do-it moments, and Calum and Caitlin, who endured many dinners of peanut butter on toast and were such excellent first readers. Thanks to Mum, Dad, Andy, Lori, Mary-Jane, Fiona, Helen, Kirsty, Sheena, Zarah and all my brilliant friends – for believing in me, even when I didn't. Also to Dr Gill Russell for help with the starry stuff, and to Dr Shelagh Neil for advice on the medical bits.

Thanks to Tallulah and Roxanne, whose enthusiasm helped me to find the best agent in the world, Darley Anderson, and also to Lucie, Julia and everyone at the agency. Last but not least, thanks to Rebecca, Francesca and the whole fab team at Puffin, for making the dream come true.

I never sleep, the night before my birthday.

It's not the usual kind of excitement – I don't get all wound up about whether I'll get a new CD player or a pair of rollerblades or a guitar. It's a guitar, anyway – Dad told me.

I'm not stressed out about a party or a sleep-over or a trip to the ice rink, either. We have this tradition, Dad and me. We stay home with a takeaway and a video. If it's his birthday, Dad picks Indian food, along with something hippy-dippy or all-action to watch, like *Lord of the Rings* or *Star Wars*. When I was little, I used to go for Disney, then soppy stuff like *The Secret Garden* or *Fairy Tale*. This year, we've got Sky TV and I get to have complete charge of the remote control all evening. I'll probably just skip between MTV and Kerrang!, munching pizza as I flick.

Birthdays are pretty cool, I know. It's just that, no matter how hard I try, I can't relax, I can't not care – and I'm always a little bit scared the night before. Every year, I'm up at dawn watching for the postman, because there's one very special card – a parcel, even, sometimes – I just *have* to get.

It's the only day of the year I hear from her.

When I was five, I got a postcard from Kathmandu. It had a picture of a Buddhist temple with a pointy golden roof and weird, staring eyes painted beneath it, and the message was written in three colours of felt pen with loads of kisses.

When I was six, there was a postcard of a donkey with flowers in its mouth, and the postmark said West Cork, Ireland. The next year I got a proper birthday card and a handmade rag doll with pink and purple hair made from fluffy yarn, and a dress stitched from somebody's old tie-dye T-shirt.

On my eighth birthday, there was a postcard from Marrakesh in Morocco, a picture of a grinning Arab girl with armfuls of gold bracelets. The next year I got a rainbow-striped hat with a floppy brim and a postcard of a castle in Wales. I wore the hat every day, till the edges got frayed and the colours ran in the wash. Then I stuck it to my pinboard, along with the postcards and the photos, and it's still there now.

When I was ten, I got a dreamcatcher, a circle

of willow criss-crossed with a crazy spider's web of bright threads and beads. Soft, white feathers hung down either side, with some tiny bells in the middle. The postcard (a spooky stone circle in Wiltshire, this time) told me to hang the dream-catcher over my bed. Its magic web would catch all my bad dreams and melt them away, so I could sleep safe and deep, all night long. Wish I'd had *that* when I was five.

Last year, when I was eleven, she sent a silver chain with a tiny chunk of rose-quartz crystal hanging from it. I always wear it, even at night. There was no postcard that year, just a letter. It's the kind of letter that's difficult to read, even now, but also the kind of letter I needed to have a long, long time ago. It said that she loved me, that she was sorry, and that one day we'd be together again.

I rolled the letter up, tied it with a strand of purple yarn from my moulting rag doll and put it in my treasure box. Then I stuck the envelope to my pinboard, so I could see her loopy, gel-pen handwriting and the postmark, which said somewhere in Cornwall. Not so very far away. But far enough.

I love my mum, but I can't really remember her. Not properly.

There are two photos of her on my pinboard.

In the first, she's standing in the rain on a

pavement in Birmingham, hand in hand with Dad. It's their wedding picture, taken just outside the registry office, twelve and a half years ago.

Mum is tiny and elfin with startling lilac-coloured hair, all braided and beaded and hanging down around her shoulders. She's wearing what looks like a lace tablecloth. It *was* a lace tablecloth, Dad told me. It cost a quid in a charity shop, and she made it into a weird, dip-hemmed number and wore it over a purple sack-dress, with purple and black stripy tights and Doc Marten boots.

Dad looks just as scary. He's so young and skinny and smiley, in patched, worn-out jeans and a vast, black mohair jumper. His hair is dyed ketchup-red, and it stands straight up as if he'd just stuck his fingers in an electric socket.

I'm in this picture, too, hidden away under the lace tablecloth. I'm just a bump, a secret, impossible to see because of the way Mum's holding her flowers (dandelions, along with some orange daisy-things pinched from the local park). All the same, I'm there, and I bet I'm the reason they're standing there in the rain, smiling at the camera and brushing confetti out of their hair.

Five months later, there I am for real, in the second photo. I'm a few weeks old, a small, angry face with black button eyes and a shock of dark hair, dressed in something bright and stripy.

Mum's face gazes up at the camera, looking pale and bewildered, her lilac hair chopped short now, tousled and scruffy. I've looked hard at that picture for signs of blissed-out motherly love and all that happy-families stuff, but Mum just looks lost, unhappy.

She left when I was four.

I don't remember, of course, but by then we'd lived in a bus, a caravan, a squat, a council flat. We toured the music festivals, Mum and Dad selling lentil soup, dreamcatchers, scented candles, handmade earrings. They worked in an organic vegetable garden, a wholefood café, a clog work-shop, a pottery. They signed on the dole and lived on social security and bought me second-hand shoes and forgot to brush my hair so it got all matted and fluffy and made old ladies at bus stops tut and shake their heads.

They tried, Dad said, to give me a name, a family, a future. She tried. *Must try harder*, like my maths teacher says.

When I was four, she ran away with a bloke called Mitch. He was taking a Volkswagen camper van to Kathmandu, and Mum must have thought that sounded better than another ten or fifteen years of wiping my nose and not brushing my hair and reading me stories about fluffy bunnies. She kissed me extra hard one night, and told me

5

she loved me, and in the morning she was gone.

We managed, Dad and me. We stayed in the council flat and I started school and he started college, doing ceramics, which is just a fancy name for pottery. I made friends with Sara and Sasha and Jade, and Dad made mugs and bowls and wiggly-edged plates all glazed with speckly stuff. He also made beautiful models of elves and fairies and sad-faced mermaids, and all of them looked a bit like Mum, but I never mentioned that.

He finished his course and we rented a place with a workshop attached, and after a while he made enough money for us to live on, selling the wiggly-edged bowls and plates to craft shops and the elfy-things to posh shops and galleries. We stopped eating lentil stew every day and progressed to French bread, oven chips and frozen vegetable lasagne, and we were happy. Mostly.

Last Christmas, Dad bought me pink flowery fairy lights, and I draped them all around my pin-board, the board where I've stuck all my postcards, along with the hat and the photos and the loved-up raggy doll.

'Looks like some kind of Hindu shrine,' Dad said when he saw it, and it does, a bit, but that's how I like it.

It's all I've got of my mum.

'Hey, Dizzy! Wake up, birthday girl!'

Dad brings me breakfast in bed on my birthday, every year. And every year, I hide under the covers and pretend I haven't been lying awake, thinking about Mum. I yawn and stretch and wipe imaginary sleep from my eyes.

The room floods with light and Dad lowers a tray laden with birthday breakfast on to the duvet. Each year, it's the same – my favourite, cheese on toast, but with a special birthday twist. Dad always layers yellow cheese over the bread, then shapes a number out of orange cheese and puts it on top to melt under the grill. This year, there are two slices of toast spelling out the fact that I'm twelve. It smells fantastic.

Dad sits down on the edge of the bed. He's skinny and mop-haired, wearing striped pyjamas and an ancient T-shirt.

'Happy birthday, Dizzy,' he grins, giving me a hug.

'Thanks, Dad.'

No more birthday blues. I bite into the toast. Happy.

There's a flower in a jam jar on the tray, and a banana milkshake, and a small, familiar parcel wrapped in blue paper. These days, I'd rather have apple juice or Coke than banana milkshake, but it was my favourite once. I tear off the blue paper and there's another old favourite, a tube of Smarties.

Everything is just the way it was the first time Dad made me a birthday breakfast, when I was five, the first birthday after Mum left. I like it like that. It's a tradition.

We share out the Smarties and Dad brings in my pressies, a couple of small parcels and something huge and guitar-shaped tied up with newspaper and Sellotape. I rip off the paper to uncover the glossy curves, wood the colour of honey and chocolate.

'Dad, it's gorgeous!' I squeal. I strum out 'Happy Birthday', slightly out of tune. My other pressies are the plum suede trainers I admired in town last week and a cool make-up bag stuffed with glittery nail varnishes. Perfect!

I'm all showered and dressed by the time the

post plops on to the mat in the hallway. I flick through the fat, pastel birthday card envelopes, looking for a postcard, a parcel, anything addressed in rainbow-coloured pen in her childish, loopy writing.

There's nothing from Mum.

After school, we pile into the window seat at Dimitri's, Jade and Sara and Sasha and me. We're all school bags, stripy ties and smiles, and Dimitri rolls his eyes as he wanders over to take the order.

'Four Cokes, please,' Sasha says, wafting a fiver.

Dimitri pretends to be shocked. Normally, we order two Cokes and four straws between us, and make them last an hour at least.

'*Four* Cokes?' he asks. 'What's the special occasion?'

'Dizzy's birthday,' Sara tells him. 'Twelve today!'

Dimitri mutters something about hopeless kids, and when the Cokes arrive I laugh, because he's loaded mine up with cocktail umbrellas, ice, lemon slices, even a huge strawberry, all floating in a sea of brown fizz.

We sip and chat and roll up our white shirt-sleeves to compare tans, because it's 18 June and summer is trying hard to burn through the grey city clouds. Sara and I are milk-bottle white, Sasha's freckly and Jade is a gorgeous golden brown, but then that doesn't count, because she always is. We decide to ditch our school trousers in favour of little skirts and ankle socks.

'How is anyone meant to look cool in school uniform?' Jade demands, dragging off her tie. 'Green with puke-yellow stripes? *Attractive*. Very.'

'Although,' Sasha says, dragging the stripy tie from Jade, 'from time to time, they *do* come in handy . . .'

I don't see it coming.

There's a quick scuffle and Sasha has the tie over my eyes. Everything goes black and there's a hand muffling my squeals and more dragging me upright. My so-called mates twirl me round three times, then there's a firm shove in the small of my back and I'm sitting again, tearing at the blindfold as they start singing 'Happy Birthday'.

The tie slides down my face and I look up, pink-cheeked. Dimitri is there, carrying four slices of hot chocolate-fudge cake with ice-cream scoops. The largest slice is stiff with pink birthday candles, flickering dangerously. There are even a few stuck in the vanilla ice.

I laugh and blush and blow out the candles and the café breaks into a sudden round of applause. I love my friends.

\*

'You've got chocolate on your nose,' Sasha tells me later, as we mooch along the street. We've linked arms and the four of us fill the pavement, high on fudge cake and the luxury of having a whole Coke each.

'I love my bracelet,' I tell her with feeling, jangling my wrist while she dabs at my nose with a tissue. 'And the CD, and the posters.' I beam at Sara and Jade.

At the traffic lights, Sara and I wave goodbye to the others and cross over, taking a short-cut through the park.

'Any postcards?' she asks quietly as we pick our way across the grass. 'Anything from . . .'

'Mum? No, not yet.'

'Well, that one from Morocco that time, you said that was late.'

'Three weeks,' I told her. 'I was only eight. I watched for the postman every morning.'

'I know,' Sara sighs.

I also cried myself to sleep every night, stopped eating, stopped talking. Then the postcard came and everything was OK again. Dad said the postal service in North Africa was probably a bit dodgy. It definitely *wasn't* Mum's fault. Not like she'd forgotten, or anything.

'Anyway,' I say brightly, 'Dad's ordering in a

pizza. Three cheese and mushroom. And I can have MTV on all night if I like.'

We leave the park, cross the road. Sara lives in a red-brick semi halfway along the street. The garden's stuffed with violently coloured flowers and the grass is so short it looks like it's been ironed.

'Coming in for a bit?' she asks.

'Nah. Pizza's calling. Thanks for the posters, Sara, I love them. See you tomorrow.'

'See ya.'

I turn away. My chirpy mood has disappeared along with Sara. There's a heavy feeling inside my chest, like I just swallowed a small iceberg and not a vast slab of hot chocolate-fudge cake. Suddenly, I feel a whole lot older than twelve.

Our flat is right down at the end of the road, a tall town house divided into three apartments. We're in the ground-floor one, so we get to use the workshop (which was once a garage) for Dad's studio. I turn into the drive and see a big, grubby van skewed across the flagstones, one front wheel squashing a straggly patch of lupins. Mr Desai from upstairs will have a fit.

It *could* be someone delivering sacks of clay for Dad, although there's no courier logo on the side. The van is mostly red with one blue wing and one grey one. One of the back doors is purple, and someone's scrawled 'wash me' in the thick grime of its window. Lovely.

I let myself into the flat. Dad's left a pile of cards from the second post on the hall table for me, and I take a deep breath before scanning it quickly.

Nothing with her handwriting.

I open the cards, trying not to feel bad. Twenty quid from Auntie Mel, a card with kittens on it from Mr Desai, a book token from Mrs Coulter, my old childminder. If they can remember, why can't she?

I can hear Dad talking to someone in the living room. I hope it's not Lucy, his girlfriend. She's OK, and I'm getting used to her, but I don't really want to share my birthday with her. Birthdays are for me and Dad.

'Home, Dad,' I shout, scooping up my post and pushing open the bedroom door. My new guitar sits proudly on the duvet. Next to it is a little blue camera from Lucy. She let me open it last night, showed me how to load the film, how to work the flash and the little zoom lens. Cool.

I dump my backpack and pull a T-shirt and jeans from the drawer.

'Dizzy?' Dad shouts back. 'Can you come through here a minute?'

I drag off my tie and wander through. It's not

Lucy. Lucy's young and smiley with fair, wavy hair. She wears wafty, trendy tops with fluted sleeves and hipsters with embroidery on them. She wears toffee-coloured lipstick and smudgy eye shadow and she smells of lime-flavoured shower gel.

This woman is older, small and tanned with smiley wrinkles and hennaed hair so short it's practically shaven. She has about a million earrings all in the same ear, as well as a stud through her right eyebrow. She's wearing weird stripy trousers that are baggy at the top and tight around the ankles, and a faded vest top with no bra underneath. Yeuchhh.

I can tell without asking she's the owner of the patchwork van, but I can't work out why she's staring so hard at me.

'Dizzy, hi,' she says, and when she grins her teeth look kind of yellow.

'Hi,' I mutter, looking at Dad for clues.

He just stares back, looking shocked and scared and flustered. He's still in his studio clothes, his jeans all streaked with clay, his hands and arms still stained reddish-brown.

'Happy birthday,' she says.

I still don't get it.

'I can't believe how much you've *grown*,' she says. 'How beautiful you are. I can't believe this is really happening . . .'

My mouth feels suddenly dry, and the floor seems to shift under my feet. I look at the tanned, smiley face with the shiny blue eyes and the glint of gold studs. I take a deep breath in, frowning.

'Hello, Mum,' I say.

It's not how I imagined.

I thought she'd be younger, more like her photos. I thought we'd run at each other and hug and hang on forever. I thought I'd be happy, not confused.

Instead, the room gets misty and my cheeks get wet and I need to sit down. Dad comes up and takes my hand, gently, leading me forwards. 'Go on,' he whispers. 'It's OK.'

And then she pulls me close. I don't want to do this, to be here. I'm stiff and wooden, silent, hostile, resisting all the way. 'It's OK, Dizzy,' she says, stroking my hair. 'It's OK.'

I take a ragged breath in, and suddenly I smell it – a rich, sweet, musty perfume from long, long ago. It's patchouli oil, the scent of my childhood.

'Oh, Mu-um . . .'

My body sways against her, my wet cheeks fall against her shoulder. We cling on, and I let the tears come, but I'm smiling, too, because I've waited so long for this moment.

It's like coming home, and I want it to go on and on.

It doesn't, of course. Too soon, she steps back, pushing me to arm's length. I wipe my eyes and nose on my sleeve, and my face feels hot and pink and swollen.

She pushes a strand of damp hair back from my face, grinning. 'Just look at the state of us! Hey, c'mon, sit down,' she says, flopping back on to the sofa. 'We have a whole load of catching up to do. And a birthday feast to plan!'

'We were going to order in a pizza,' Dad chips in. 'Three cheese and mushroom. Want to share, or would you like something different?'

Mum frowns. 'Not pizza,' she says. 'I'm vegan these days, didn't I tell you? No cheese, no milk, no eggs, no honey.'

'Right,' says Dad, looking lost again.

'Besides,' Mum is saying. 'This is a special occasion. Why don't we make miso soup and red bean stew and maybe muesli cake for afters? We can all help. Sound OK, Dizzy?'

'Sure,' I nod, not understanding a word of it. 'Fine.'

'Well, I can ask if they'll do a pizza with no cheese and lots of extra topping,' Dad suggests.

'Pizza's kind of a tradition on Dizzy's birthday.'

'No, no,' I say quickly. 'Bean stew would be great. Honest, Dad.'

Actually, I hate kidney beans, and Dad knows that. Muesli cake sounds more like hamster bedding than food, and I haven't a clue what miso soup is, but if your mum turned up on your birthday after eight years' absence, wouldn't *you* be trying to please her?

'We'll be here all night,' Dad mutters, heading over to the open-plan kitchen.

'So?' she shrugs. 'We'll be here all night. What's the big deal?'

And because my mum has just told me she'll be here all night, and that means she won't be leaving for the next half-hour at least, I hug her again. 'Mum,' I say into her velvet hair. 'I've missed you so-o-o much!'

'Hey, hey!' she laughs, wriggling free. 'I've missed you too, babe. Only don't call me *Mum*, OK? It makes me feel about a hundred and three. Call me Storm.'

I know from Dad that she was christened Linda Caroline Tanner, and when they got married she became Linda Caroline Kerr, but Linda's no name for a punk, a rebel, a New Age traveller.

When I was a toddler, she reinvented herself as Storm. Just Storm. I might do the same thing

18

when I'm older, only I'll ditch Dizzy for something plain and simple and ordinary, like Jane or Ann or Mary.

*Storm*, though. Dad said she chose it because it was strong and brave and unstoppable, but it always makes me think of hailstones, thunder, gale-force winds.

'Storm, then.' The name feels strange in my mouth.

In the kitchen, Dad is boiling a pan of water and washing rice over the sink. He grabs a bag of stir-fry veg from the freezer and heats the wok.

'Need any help?' Storm calls over.

'No, no, you two just relax,' Dad says. 'Everything's under control.'

He tips rice into the pan, tears open the stir-fry and adds it to the sizzling wok. He roots in a cupboard for a jar of curry sauce.

'Is that vegan?' Storm asks. 'Can you check the label?'

'It's fine,' Dad promises, but Storm goes over to check it anyhow.

'All these chemicals and E-numbers,' she says, wrinkling up her nose. 'You should buy organic, Pete. There's just no goodness left in this at all.'

'Tastes good, though,' Dad winks at me.

'Well, it's Dizzy's treat, I suppose,' she concedes. 'Look, if you won't let me help, at least let me contribute something. I think there's some bits and pieces in the van.'

It's weird, because the minute she goes out of the room my heart twists, like it's scared she's leaving me all over again. Dad looks over and catches me chewing my lip.

'Go and see if she needs a hand,' he suggests, and I wonder how he always knows exactly the right thing to say.

Years of practice, probably.

I wander outside and peer in through the van's open purple door. Inside it's a mad, multi-coloured nest of quilts and cushions. All down one side are kitchen cupboards, painted with swirls and spirals and crescent moons. A big bundle of long, skinny twigs lies the whole length of the van's floor. Weirdest of all, tucked into the corner, there's a tiny cast-iron stove with a long chimney-pipe that juts right out the top of the roof.

You could *live* in this van. It looks like Storm does.

Strings of bells are looped across the ceiling, and they jingle as she brushes against them, heaving down a brightly woven shoulder bag and a rolled-up quilt. She reaches under the tiny sink and pulls out a big jar of cloudy amber liquid with a hand-drawn label.

'Scrumpy,' she grins at me. 'For your dad. It'll loosen him up a bit.'

'Right.'

In the house, Storm unrolls the purple quilt and spreads it out across the sofa, making it look suddenly exotic. She sits back down and folds her legs up beneath her, reaching deep into the rucksack. 'Carob,' she announces, pulling out a slab of dirt-coloured stuff wrapped up in foil. 'Try it.'

I take a bite. It tastes like soil, only less appealing. 'Excellent,' I nod.

'Now . . . where are they? Ah!' She brings out a small package swathed in black velvet. Carefully, she opens out the cloth to reveal a pack of cards tied up with gold cord. They're not hearts, diamonds, spades or clubs.

'Tarot cards,' says Storm.

'What are they?' I ask, stroking the bright cards as she swirls them face-down across the carpet. 'What do they do?'

Storm grins. 'The tarot are ancient, fortune-telling cards with a magic all their own,' she tells me. 'Fancy a glimpse of the future, Dizz?'

4

There's a kind of row about whether Storm should do my tarot cards or not. Dad says it's superstitious rubbish and Storm says, in that case, what's the problem? It's just a bit of fun.

She pours him a mug of scrumpy and tells him it's extra-strong cider brewed by a mad old bloke in Somerset. Dad rolls his eyes, but takes a drink anyway, and Storm spreads out the tarot pack and gets me to pick some cards.

It may be just a bit of fun, but when Storm says that my calm, cautious, ordered life is about to change forever, I feel a tingle down my spine. The cards predict adventure, travel, freedom.

'Kids *need* calm and caution and order,' Dad says.

'No, Pete, look at this,' she insists. 'The end of childhood. She's at a crossroads in her life. I see new opportunities, the healing of old wounds. She will choose the path that's least expected.'

'I don't *think* so,' he snorts.

'Dad, please,' I beg. 'Storm, what does it mean? What's going to happen?'

Dad stalks over and knocks the cards to the floor, his face a tight mask of anger.

'Just *stop* it, Storm,' he snaps. 'These are our lives you're playing with here. It's not a game.'

Storm shrugs and gathers up the cards, tying them back safely inside the gold cord and hiding them in the folds of black velvet. 'Did I say it was a game?' she whispers.

We eat vegetable curry and brown rice (no red beans), and Storm says it's lovely, in spite of the bottled sauce. She tops up Dad's mug of scrumpy.

'So,' he asks her coolly. 'What are your plans? Don't tell me you were just passing by, eight years on, and thought you'd call in and say hi.'

'Dad!'

Storm smiles, sadly. 'You're right, of course,' she says. 'I can understand why you're so suspicious. I've hurt you both, I know, but I had my reasons, Dizzy, I promise you. There's so much you'll never know. And there's not a day gone past when I haven't thought of you with love.'

She puts a hand out to stroke my cheek, and instantly my eyes mist over.

'Spare us the heartache,' Dad laughs. 'You could have visited, or phoned, or written.'

But she did write, every year. Doesn't he know how much that meant to me? I know he's only angry because she hurt him, but she hurt me too, didn't she? If I can forgive her, why can't he?

Storm sighs. 'Dizzy and I have a lot of catching up to do,' she admits. 'But, Pete, I'm here because I want to try. I *wasn't* just passing by – I've driven over 200 miles to see my daughter on her special day.'

My heart just about flips over.

The phone starts ringing out in the hall, but nobody moves to answer it. The answerphone clicks on, and I hear Sasha reminding me I need my gym kit tomorrow for the basketball try-outs.

'I want to put things right, make up for the past,' Storm rushes on. 'It's summer now, school holidays and all that. I want Dizzy to come with me for a bit – a break, a holiday, whatever. We can do some mother–daughter bonding, get to know each other properly. We can take in a few festivals, go to the coast, just the two of us.'

'Oh, *Mum*!' I squeal. 'Storm, I mean. I'd *love* that. It's what I've always dreamed of.'

Well, actually, I dreamed that Mum would come home and we'd all live together in the flat, but this is close enough. It's a start.

'*No!*'

Dad slams his plate down so hard it skids across

the floorboards, scattering rice and baby sweetcorn as it goes.

'*No,*' he says again. 'You think you can just stroll back into our lives and hurt us all over again? No, Linda, Storm, whatever you want to call yourself. You *can't.*

'Dizzy has five more weeks of school – she can't just take off and disappear. She has a school concert and a swimming gala and end-of-year tests. You are not going to drag her all over the country to live in some ancient van and eat nettle soup and hang out with losers. No *way.*'

There's a long silence. Storm gathers up the plates, including Dad's, and takes them across to the sink. She runs them under the cold tap and dumps them in the drainer. There's a streak of curry sauce still sticking to one, but I daren't say so.

I look down, and my cheeks burn pink.

'Dizzy?' Dad says.

I glance up slowly, but I can't quite meet his eye.

'Dizzy, maybe when school closes you could go for a week or so. We both could. But not now. Seriously, no *way.*'

Storm pours another mug of cider for Dad. If he doesn't slow down, he's going to be drunk as well as grumpy. I notice Storm is sticking to water. It's probably something to do with being a vegan.

'Let's not argue, Pete,' she says mildly. 'It was only an idea.'

'It was in the tarot, though,' I chip in.

'I don't care if it was in the *Sunday Mirror*,' Dad scowls.

'No rows,' Storm says again. 'I just thought that Dizzy might like to come to this little solstice gathering in Wales, a really magical place, all hills and streams, and only a few special friends. But if your dad says no . . .'

'Don't be making out it's all *my* fault!' Dad roars. 'You started this, Storm. Look, I've said we can meet up some time in the holidays, but that's not good enough, is it? You always have to get your own way. D'you think I don't remember that?'

This is *not* the way it's meant to happen. In my head, Storm comes back all apologetic and sad and says she's had enough of the open road. She starts acting like other people's mums, making chocolate traybakes, picking me up from basketball practice, coming to Parents' Evening.

Scary thought.

I can live with the earrings and the stud and the weird clothes, and I can just about handle the van (she could always get a respray). I can even cope with the carob and the bean stew, but all this fighting *has* to stop. Dad's meant to be pleased to see her. He's spent long enough pining for her, hasn't he? What's going on?

'I've got a maths test tomorrow,' I say quietly, getting to my feet. 'Think I'll go have a look. Don't want to flunk out or anything.'

Dad frowns. 'Dizzy, sweetheart, don't go,' he says. 'What about MTV? And there's toffee pop-corn in the cupboard. We're not really arguing, y'know, just talking things through.'

Yeah, right.

Storm follows me out into the hall.

'I'm sorry,' I whisper. 'I don't know why he's being so awkward. He's not usually like this.'

She raises one eyebrow, the one with the stud. 'Do you *want* to come?' she asks.

'Course I do!'

'Then don't worry,' she says. 'Just relax. It's going to happen. Just leave it to me . . .'

It's still dark, but Storm is shaking me gently, dragging me back from my dreams.

'Dizz, *quickly*, we can't hang about. We've got a long way to drive.'

'Hmmm?'

'Dizzy, come *on*,' she whispers. 'You need to pack.'

I sit up, feeling dazed.

'What are you doing?'

Storm upends my rucksack, dumping school books, jotters and gym kit all over the floor. She pulls out the drawers of my dressing table, fishing out socks and undies and T-shirts and jeans, jamming the lot into the rucksack. She scoops up a random mess of bracelets, scrunchies, combs and gel from the top of the dresser, then looks up at the pinboard.

'Hey,' she says. 'Didn't I give you that rag doll?'

'When I was seven,' I tell her, padding across the carpet to stand beside her.

The doll is pinned up by the neck of her faded, tie-dye frock, her fluffy lilac hair thin and grimy now. I called her Linda Caroline, after Mum.

'You kept it, all this time,' she says softly.

I wait for her to see the postcards, the photos, the scuddy old hat, but she doesn't seem to notice them. Maybe they're not all that memorable, except to me.

'Why are we packing? Did Dad change his mind?'

Storm grins at me, her dark eyes twinkling. 'It's sorted,' she laughs. 'All organized, no hassles. I've always been able to wind Pete round my little finger!'

It didn't sound that way last night, but who am I to argue? If she's got Dad to agree I can skive off school for five weeks, it's nothing short of a miracle.

'What did he say? What about the concert and the tests and the gala? Is he going to phone the school? Storm, how did you *do* it?'

She holds a finger to her lips, still grinning. 'Trust me,' she whispers. 'And *c'mon*, pack!'

'OK, OK . . . I just want to see Dad first. Say thanks!'

'Not yet,' Storm hisses. 'It's only five in the morning, he's fast asleep. And he had a skinful last night, I bet he's got a massive hangover. That scrumpy has a real kick to it.'

'Well, later, then,' I frown. 'I'll make him a coffee.'

'Whatever. Just *pack*!'

I wash quickly and pull on purple bleach-dye cords and a stripy top. I brush my hair and plait it into two heavy ropes (when I leave it loose it just gets frizzy and annoying). I pack the hairbrush and root around in the bottom of my wardrobe for a couple of big jumpers, last winter's boots, flip-flops and my new plum suede trainers.

I pocket the twenty quid from Auntie Mel's card, pack my new camera, zip my guitar into its travel case. I hunt down nail scissors, a towel, a big bottle of Orange Zest Shampoo.

Storm laughs. 'Where did I get *you* from?' she says, shaking her head. 'You'll be packing an iron and a first-aid kit, next! We're going to do the festivals, Dizzy – ease up, travel light! And no hair-dryer, OK?'

'OK.'

In the kitchen, the big jug of cider is almost empty. Ouch. Dad doesn't drink much usually, so I bet he's got a really sore head this morning. I put the kettle on for his coffee.

Storm's raiding the fridge for travel snacks. I notice her stash away orange juice, butter, cheese, coleslaw, yoghurts. 'Well, *you're* not vegan, are you?' she says defensively. 'Anyway, Pete won't mind. Hurry up, now, it's almost six – we need to get moving.'

'Right. I'll just take Dad his coffee.'

'Right. But Dizzy, listen – don't make a big deal of it, OK? We don't want him to change his mind. Don't go on about missing him and stuff, it's not like we're going to be away for long . . .'

'No, sure,' I agree. 'But I have to see him, y'know? I have to say goodbye.'

Storm shrugs and goes back to ransacking the fridge.

Dad's room stinks of curry and cider. The air is thick and stale and heavy, and Dad's asleep with the duvet over his head and his feet sticking out over the side of the bed. He forgot to take his socks off.

'Dad? Dad, wake up!' I hiss, peeling back the duvet and shaking his shoulder. He's fully dressed, yesterday's T-shirt crumpled and grubby.

'Gnnnhh?'

He groans and tries to hide under the pillow.

'Dad, Dad, listen,' I tell him. 'I just wanted to say thanks. I can't believe you changed your mind, but I'm so, *so-oo* happy. Thanks, Dad.'

I hug him, breathing in sweat and scrumpy and curry and clay.

31

'Urggh . . . mouth feels like the bottom of a bird-cage,' he moans. 'That scrumpy's evil stuff. My head . . .'

'Never mind. I made you a coffee.'

He props himself up on one elbow, wincing at the effort. His eyes are all screwed up against the light and his hair is sticking out in clumps. His hand shakes a bit as he takes the coffee, so I take it back again and put it down on the bedside table.

He's looking kind of *green*.

'Good birthday, then?' he says in a wobbly voice, covering his eyes.

'The best ever,' I promise. 'The guitar, then Mum, now . . . this!'

'Hmmfff?'

'Seriously, Dad, you are *totally* the best. I'll never be able to thank you enough. Look, I have to get going, now. You sleep in, take a lazy day, you deserve it. I'm gonna miss you . . .'

Oops. Storm told me not to get all soppy.

'OK, see you later, sweetheart,' Dad says with an effort, burrowing down under the covers again.

I pause in the doorway. I want another hug, a proper chat, a long goodbye, but Dad's snoring gently. I close the door and creep away.

An hour later, we're rattling along at forty-five miles an hour in the patchwork van. My bags and my guitar are in the back, cocooned in quilts, and we're scoffing Mars bars from Hilton Park service station, where we pulled in for a fuel and toilet stop.

'Not exactly vegan,' Storm admits. 'But this *is* a special occasion!'

I'm sitting up front, looking out at the open road over a dashboard draped with tinsel and bells and Blu-tacked seashells. A clump of dried flowers, ribbons and feathers dangles from the roof, swinging from side to side.

We've just turned off the motorway, heading north. The van rattles and coughs like it's tied together with string, and Storm says we're safer sticking to smaller roads in case we get pulled by the police.

'When d'you think we'll be in Wales?' I ask.

'Well . . .'

Storm takes a skinny, handrolled ciggy from her bag and makes a big production of lighting it with a red plastic lighter. She takes a few deep draws.

'Don't mind, do you?' she asks, grinning.

'No, course not,' I say.

'So. Did I say Wales, last night?' she goes on. 'Must be getting forgetful, Dizz. I meant *Scotland*. The solstice festival's in Scotland, up in the mountains. I can't believe I said *Wales*.'

'Doesn't matter.'

'Well, you know, it's just a tiny gathering, just us and some really good friends. Like a little family, yeah?'

I bite my lip. Wales, Scotland, it doesn't make much difference.

'OK, babe?' Storm asks. 'You're kind of quiet.'

'I'm fine. I was just thinking . . .'

'Yeah?'

I frown. 'Well, when I said bye to Dad earlier on . . .'

Storm snaps to attention. 'What is it? What did he say?'

'Well, nothing much,' I admit. 'He was sort of hung-over, like you said. But – well, when I said I was going, he just said *see you later*, like I was off to school or something. Does that seem . . . a bit weird, to you?'

'Maybe he didn't want to make a fuss,' says Storm.

'Maybe.'

'Or – I remember now. He said he'll try and meet up with us in a week or two. Stick around for a bit. It'll be like old times!'

'Oh . . . that's *great*.' I let out a long sigh of relief. 'Where's he going to meet us? When?'

Storm stubs out her roll-up on the jingly dashboard.

'Oh, he said he'd come up to the Tree People

Festival in a week or two. Don't stress, Dizz, I'll let him know where we are.'

A warm, happy glow seeps through my body, and I stretch back in my seat. I can't stop smiling.

'Sorry,' I tell Storm. 'I keep having to pinch myself to remember I'm not dreaming. It's just too good to be true. For a minute there, I started wondering if Dad got mixed up about the holiday, if he agreed maybe when he was drunk and then didn't remember . . .'

Storm rakes about in the glove compartment and drags out an old music tape, squinting at it as she drives. 'You worry too much,' she says, distractedly. 'Pete knows you're with me, and I'm your *mum*, aren't I? What's the problem?'

'No problem!'

She shoves the tape into the cassette deck and a jiggy, rackety noise erupts, almost drowning out the van's roar.

'This afternoon we'll be on a Scottish hillside, with wildflowers under our feet and nothing but blue skies above us. Just you and me, Dizz. No school, no rules, no worries, no hassles, just nature and music and peace and fun. How cool is that?'

Pretty cool.

You learn something new every day, Dad says. Most days, it's French verbs and algebra and the life cycle of the frog, but today is different.

Today I'm learning about the most important day of the whole traveller year, the solstice. It all starts tomorrow, 20 June, and guess what? I'm on my way to a solstice festival to celebrate. The night of 20 June is the shortest night of the year. The sun doesn't set till almost eleven, and then it rises next day at four in the morning.

Storm says that the summer solstice is when the earth's energies are at their strongest. It's a magical night, she says, a night when the curtain between the world of man and the world of nature is at its thinnest. It's a night when dreams come true, when anything can happen.

We're going to take lanterns up to the top of the hill and sing and dance and stay up all night to see the sun rise. I've never done that before.

'Things are changing for you, Dizz,' Storm says. 'I saw it in your cards. It's time to ease up, relax, live a little. Have fun, yeah?'

'Yeah.'

'Anyway, we're *nearly* there.'

The track is so rough and steep and pot-holey, I think the patchwork van will probably collapse and die right here, right now. We're bumping along at ten miles an hour and the engine is howling in pain, but Storm just smokes and smiles and steers the van onwards.

Every bone in my body feels bashed and broken by the time we arrive at the field marked 'car park'. We veer off the track and crash down across the rutted ground, and Storm squeezes the van in among an unruly tangle of ancient buses, vans and cars.

'So,' she grins. 'This is it! Grab your bags and one of those quilts and we'll get moving.'

I look around for nature, music, peace and fun, but all I can see are dusty old junkyard wrecks and a lone sheep peering over the wall at me. I struggle into my rucksack, sling the holdall over one shoulder, my guitar over the other, then try to wrestle a rolled-up quilt into submission. Storm laughs. She drags the quilt-roll off me, flings it over her shoulder and picks up the carrier bags of supplies we bought two hours back in a super-market in Carlisle.

We trail up a smaller, steeper track, through a wood full of tiny, twisty trees with branches that reach out to us like fingers. My legs start to ache and the rucksack drags and the holdall keeps slipping off my shoulder.

In the distance, I hear a slow, soft drumbeat. Thin squeals and dipping voices float down towards us. As we come to the edge of the woods, I see the tepees, three towering canvas structures, surrounded by countless smaller tents.

Bright, ragbag people sit around the clearing, talking, smoking, laughing. A posse of skinny mon-grel dogs scrounge around a scruffy child eating white bread straight from the packet. The smell of wood smoke fills my nose, familiar, comforting.

'I remember that smell,' I whisper.

Storm laughs. 'Well, of course you do, Dizz! You spent the first four years of your life at festivals like this one, didn't you? You're going to love it.'

I don't love it, though, as we walk across the clearing, all eyes fixed on us, interested, welcoming, curious. It's worse than reading out loud in assem-bly, all those faces, a few arms raised in greeting. My heart thumps louder than the drumbeat, and my cheeks flame.

Suddenly, from nowhere, a big black-and-white dog charges straight at us, yelping, squealing, circling around. It jumps up at Storm and she swats it away, laughing, but when it leaps at me I'm terrified. I stagger backwards, dropping my bags and my guitar. Its face is long and thin and hairy, with sharp teeth and slavering jaws like a piebald wolf.

'Leggit!' Storm shouts, and the dog subsides, but not before it's stabbed me in the stomach with its claws. My eyes prickle with tears, and I have to bite my lip to keep them back, bending to rescue my guitar.

'She didn't mean it, love,' a plump, dark-haired woman says, grabbing hold of the dog's collar. 'She's just a big daft pup.'

The dog is still writhing about in excitement, trying to lick my hands. I can see now it didn't mean any harm and I feel embarrassed.

'I'm not used to dogs,' I say.

'You will be,' Storm says. 'OK, Leggit, OK. Bloody pest.'

She drops her bags and quilt on the grass outside one of the tepees.

'This is Tess,' Storm gestures to the plump woman. 'She's known you since you were – oh, well, since forever, I suppose. She made that rag doll you've got at home.'

'Oh!'

It's not much of a greeting, but it's all I can manage. I thought *Storm* had made that doll. I thought . . .

'Nice to meet you again, Dizzy,' Tess says. 'Don't suppose you remember Finn?' She points across the clearing, where a sulky teenage boy in a black hoodie and filthy frayed jeans is standing, hands in pockets, staring. As our eyes meet, he turns away.

'Used to be inseparable, you two did. Still, that was a long time ago. This must all seem pretty strange . . .'

'No, I . . .'

'Hey, Storm!'

A tall man is striding across the clearing, tanned and lean with frizzy fair hair, flecks of gold stubble on his jaw and eyes like chips of green ice. He's carrying an armful of wood, big logs and curving branches that trail along the grass behind him. A small boy; mousy, colourless, follows behind, carrying smaller, twiggy branches.

They ditch their haul beside a vast, central logpile, but Storm doesn't wait for them to come towards us. She launches herself at the man, flinging her arms around him. They kiss, and I have to look away.

'That's Zak,' Tess says. 'She tell you about him?'

I shake my head.

'He's OK,' Tess says. 'The little boy's called Mouse.'

My stomach lurches suddenly, and my mouth feels dry.

'Is he . . . I mean, is Mouse . . .'

'Oh, *no*,' Tess laughs. 'No, Mouse is *Zak's* son. He's only been with us a few weeks, he used to live with his mum. He'll settle down.'

She lets go of the dog's collar and it leaps away, circling Zak and Storm, its tail thrashing. Mouse has disappeared.

I sink down on to the grass, cradling my guitar. My face aches, frozen into a smile. I'm waiting for someone to tell me what to do, how to act. I'm waiting for Storm to remember I'm here.

I wish I'd never come.

I lie in my sleeping bag staring up into the tall, tapering roof of the tepee, where the long larch poles cross. Last night the smoke from the fire rose in a thick, choking plume, up and out through the gap in the canvas above me. Now the fire is sleeping, a mound of ash and cinders with a few blackened beer cans at the edge.

A dozen or more people were packed in here last night, laughing, eating, drinking, smoking. They sat around the fire, people with tie-dyed shirts and patched jeans, rainbow sweaters, trailing crinkly skirts, baggy trousers, skintight vests. I didn't have time to be shy.

Tess dished out potato stew from a huge cauldron. I passed round the bread – we used up two whole loaves, plus a slab of cheddar and the bag of supermarket apples Storm had bought earlier. Then cans of beer and bottles of cider appeared and a man with a white beard started playing the fiddle, and the air was thick with songs and smoke and laughter.

It was gone midnight when the party eased up. People stood up, drunkenly, hugging each other good night before lurching off into the dark. A few people just curled up where they were, dragging quilts and blankets out from along the edge of the tepee, even though they had their own tents out there somewhere.

I heard Mouse creep in long after everyone was asleep – everyone but me. I heard him pick his way through the sleeping bodies, a tiny shadow in the dark. He curled up next to Leggit, the skinny lurcher, and pulled a corner of someone else's red blanket over his body. Later, much later, I thought I heard him whimper in the dark, but I can't be sure.

He's gone, now. No Leggit, no Mouse, and the man with the red blanket turns out to be the white-bearded wrinkly with the fiddle. I wonder if he knows he snores? On the other side of the tepee, Storm and Zak lie wrapped around each other, a muddle of arms and legs and patchwork quilt. I can't look at them. It's not like I expected Storm was going to come home and live happily ever after with Dad. Not really. But still, it's hard to look.

My watch says four thirty and daylight streams

in through the pale canvas walls. My guitar hangs from a loop of rope tied round one of the larch poles. The inside of the tepee is draped with cloth, hung with bags, supermarket carriers, four-packs of beer. Yesterday, Storm showed me how to loop, hook and hang my stuff up out of the way.

It's not the first time I've slept in a tepee. Storm says we've done it before, when I was little, at festivals like this. A tepee is a magical place to live, because it's round, it has no corners. Everyone is equal.

They're sleeping soundly, making little fluttery sounds, coughing, snoring. I lie wide awake, stiff and terrified, scared to make a sound.

I don't belong. I want my own bed, my own bedroom. I want my dad.

If I got up now I could walk through the sleeping festival, down the hillside. I could walk along the country lanes until I found a village with a phone box and I could call my dad. He'd come and fetch me, and we'd be home by teatime, curled up, eating pizza and joking about how the tarot is never wrong.

I know I won't, though. I *won't* run away.

Quietly, so as not to wake the muddle of sleepers, I slither free of my sleeping bag. I slept in my clothes and boots, so I stand up creakily, picking a path between the bodies. Accidentally, I kick the fiddle-case, and the old beardy guy sits bolt upright, glaring around fiercely.

'Sorry,' I whisper, but the old bloke's eyes are milky with sleep. He looks right through me.

I duck out through the doorflap, blinking in the thin green light that filters through the trees. The camp is silent. The air smells sharp and new. A few birds skitter through the tree tops, their song drifting down across the empty clearing.

Last night was noisy and hassled and I was way out of my depth, but this morning it's fresh and clean, like anything is possible.

Almost anything.

I wander through the tents, avoiding guy-ropes and empty bottles and the blackened, crackled wood from a dozen cooking fires. Beyond the tents, the woods are cool and green. I step through curls of soft green bracken and my boots crunch twigs, squelch into damp, mossy hollows.

I remember the kids' story about a brother and sister who leave a trail of breadcrumbs to help them find their way back home through the forest. The birds flutter down and eat the breadcrumbs and the children are lost.

I leave no trail.

Instead of a gingerbread house, I find a stream, a tiny, ice-white slash of water, cutting through the trees. The water is fast, pushing past the rocks with a froth of creamy surf. I think of the stand-pipe in the camp clearing where I filled a kettle for Tess last night, and wonder how many of the festival-goers know this is even here.

Some do.

A makeshift den of fallen branches sits by the water's edge. As I creep closer, hardly daring to breathe, I see bracken, moss and black bin bags woven in and out of the branches, as well as feathers, twigs, grass and gobbets of dried mud. Dead matches lie scattered across the ground, among the embers of a little bonfire.

Inside, there's a dirty sleeping bag, a chocolate wrapper and a grey-fur toy mouse, streaked with dirt. A ragged black-and-white heap of spiky hair and bones lies huddled beside it, and two grey eyes blink at me from the shadows, black ears flopping to attention.

'Shhh . . .' I whisper, offering my hand to be sniffed.

The wolf-dog snuffles lazily, painting my hand with a warm, wet tongue before settling itself down again.

The sleeping bag stirs, curling, rustling. A tousled head appears briefly, eyes screwed tight shut against the light, before dipping back out of sight. A skinny arm snakes over the sleeping bag and blackened fingers close round the toy mouse.

Mouse and Leggit have a place all of their own.

I move away quietly, following the water downstream until the den is out of sight over my shoulder. Then I kneel down beside the stream and plunge my fingers into the icy flow, scooping up handfuls of silvery water to splash my face. The cold makes me gasp, and my skin tingles. There's nothing to dry myself on, so the water drips down my neck. A couple of ratty bits of hair, escaped from yesterday's plaits, cling in dark, wet ringlets around my face.

'Bet *that* woke you up.'

I blink, wiping droplets of water from my lashes.

To my right, a huge old oak tree spreads its branches out across the stream. Finn sits astride the lowest branch, his legs swinging. He grins, then looks away into the distance, his face dappled green in the dawn light. He doesn't look like a sulky teenager any more, just a big kid in tattered skate clothes.

'It's freezing,' I say, which may well be my stupidest comment ever. Like a mountain stream was ever going to be *warm*.

Finn rolls on to his stomach and lowers himself down from the oak branch. He hangs for a moment, bare feet peeking out from frayed, baggy jeans. Then he drops and turns to me.

He's older than me, maybe thirteen or fourteen. He's really tanned and his eyes are a surprising blue-grey colour. Jade, who knows about these things, would say he's good-looking. I like his hair, which is dark and thick and matted into dread-locks, reaching almost to his shoulders.

'You don't remember me, do you?' he says.

'Not really.'

'I s'pose it was a long time ago. We used to meet up at the festivals, your family and mine. Storm and Tess were good mates – still are. You were just a baby, really, but you always wanted to be doing what the other kids were doing. You were always following me, tagging along.'

'Sorry,' I say. 'Must have been a pain.'

Finn laughs. 'Not really,' he says. 'I kind of liked it. You were always asking questions, always listen-ing, like I was the smartest kid you ever met. It made me feel important. I suppose I thought you were kind of cute.'

'Oh!'

'Long time ago, though,' Finn says again, in case I might be getting any ideas.

'Sure.'

'D'you see Mouse up there?' he asks, poking one bare toe into the water. Barefoot, in the woods? Ouch.

'Yeah – he's asleep in the den with that scruffy dog.'

'Right. He doesn't much like the tepee, or the festival. He's missing his mum,' Finn says. He steps into the stream, letting the frayed hems of his jeans soak up water like blotting paper. I can see his toes, pale and bluish, curved around a rock beneath the rushing water.

'Coming in?'

I shake my head. 'No *way*. Too cold – I tried it already, remember?'

'Chicken,' Finn says, kicking an arc of water towards me.

'Don't!' I squeal, pulling at my splattered cords. I take a shaky step towards him, balancing on a shiny rock midstream. I dip the toe of my boot into the water to get my revenge, but the movement wrecks my balance and I slide off the rock into the water, screaming, laughing.

Icy water floods my boots, soaks my socks. My feet slide over the rocks on the streambed, and it's only when Finn grabs at my elbow that I manage to stand upright.

'I changed my mind,' I tell him, as we stagger, giggling, towards the bank.

'Sure,' laughs Finn, 'sure you did. Only next time, Dizzy, remember you're supposed to take off your boots!'

49

I drag myself up out of the water, boots squelching.

'I will,' I tell him. 'Next time, I'll remember.'

So, I've made a friend. Unbelievably, he's a male friend. Sara, Sasha and Jade would be speechless.

OK, so they might not approve of his dusty, felted dreadlocks or his dirty fingernails or the faint grey tidemark that edges his jaw, but so what? They're not here and Finn is, and right now I need a friend. Especially a friend I've known since forever, even if there has been an eight-year gap in the relationship.

We sit on the bank, with our feet turning blue in the water, and we talk. Finn tells me about his mum, Tess, and his dad, some old Irish hippy he never knew. He tells me about his brother, Niall, who's just finished his A levels and chose to stay home in Lancashire because he's grown out of festivals.

'Will you grow out of them, too?' I ask.

Finn shrugs. 'Right now it's OK. I get to skive off school for a while and bum around the country-side. I'm no crusty, though. I'm not going to waste *my* life sitting in a tepee smoking dope and talking about all the stuff I'll never get around to doing.'

My heart thuds.

'Last night . . . that was *dope* they were smoking?'

Finn laughs. 'You really haven't been around festivals for a while, have you?' he grins. 'Yes, Dizzy, of course it was dope. Y'know, spliff, weed, whatever you want to call it. You were probably half-stoned yourself, sitting in there breathing all that smoke.'

'But –' I struggle to get things straight. 'Isn't it – isn't that *drugs*? Isn't that illegal?'

Finn rolls his eyes. 'Yes, it's drugs,' he says. 'Yes, it's illegal. The papers are always going on about how it's no worse than drink or tobacco, but it's still against the law. Bet you never knew your mum was an outlaw, did you?'

I flop back into the grass. There's a lot I didn't know about my mum. A lot I still don't know. I feel angry, embarrassed, ashamed.

'Look, Dizzy, it's a hippy thing, a festival thing,' Finn says. 'I didn't mean to upset you.'

'You didn't,' I lie.

'I did. I'm sorry,' he says.

I shut my eyes and try not to care. How am I meant to know stuff like this, anyway?

I know about drugs, of course. We've had lessons at school about what to do if your friend offers you something dodgy. You just say no, and you try not to judge them, but it's OK to tell a teacher all the same, because drugs are dangerous, they can wreck your life.

I shudder. Nobody ever told us at school what you're meant to do if your *mum* offers you weed. Well, she hasn't, not yet, but you never know. It could happen.

'Isn't it really bad for you?' I ask at last. 'Dangerous? That's what they say at school.'

Finn frowns, flicking pebbles into the stream one by one. 'Dunno,' he considers. 'Weed's not like the really bad things, heroin and crack and all that. I think they just do it to relax.'

'Do you smoke it? Weed, I mean?' I ask Finn.

'Me? No *way*,' he answers. 'I hate all that. They smoke and they laugh and they talk about all these brilliant ideas they've got. Storm and Zak are always going on about this healing centre they want to set up in India or Spain. Well, they can dream, that's fine. Only they'll never *do* it, and you know why? Because they just smoke and talk and forget it all in the morning.

'I used to believe in the stories, I used to get excited, think we really *would* go to live in a commune on a Greek island or start up an animal sanctuary. It's just daydreams, though. It doesn't mean anything.'

Finn chucks a big, craggy rock into the stream, and we watch the ripples spread as it sinks and disappears without trace. I don't say anything.

'I hate weed,' Finn says. 'It makes you lazy. It makes you sit around dreaming when you could be out there doing something practical to make your dreams come true. I mean, festivals are OK. They're fun. But don't get me wrong – I want more out of life than *this*.'

'Me, too,' I say, although I haven't a clue what I want. It seems to change every other minute, and for now, having Finn like me and not rate me a total loser is pretty high on my wish list.

'It's not like they're doing any harm,' he says eventually. 'Well, only to themselves. They're just turning slowly from New Age travellers into *Old* Age travellers.'

We sit in silence, the stream rushing past us.

'I don't really know Storm at all,' I say, thinking out loud.

Finn looks at me, and I can't read the expression in his blue-grey eyes. It might be sympathy, or understanding, or even pity. 'No,' he says softly. 'I don't suppose you do.'

Then he jumps up, brushing down his soggy jeans. 'I'm starving,' he declares. 'Let's go see if there's any breakfast going.'

Back at the camp, people are beginning to stir.

Little Calor gas stoves hiss beneath battered kettles, blackened pans of baked beans sit heating among the sticks of the morning's newly lit fires. There's a knot of sleepy-faced women chatting beside the tap, and assorted toddlers drift across the grass, eating bread and honey or hunks of cheese while the mongrel dogs hover, ever hopeful.

Finn takes me to the big red family tent he shares with Tess, and there's Mouse, finishing off a tin plate of scrambled eggs, wiping it clean with a wedge of bread. Next to him, Leggit, the black-and-white wolf-dog, is lapping water from a plastic bowl and crunching dog biscuits straight from the carton.

Mouse looks at us warily from big, brown eyes, his face pinched and hostile. Finn ruffles his hair and sits down, but Mouse pulls away, scowling. He shoots a furious look at me, too, dropping his plate on to the grass and edging away from the tent like he can't work out whether to hate us or be scared of us.

'See you later, Mouse,' Tess calls lightly as the small, skinny figure slopes off, disappearing in the muddle of tents.

'I don't think he likes me very much,' I say.

'I don't think he likes *any* of us very much,' Finn agrees. 'Except Tess, and that's probably because she remembers to feed him. And Leggit, because the two of them curl up together at night. He must be feeling rotten.'

'Poor kid,' Tess nods darkly.

Finn dishes up a plate of scrambled eggs and hands it to me, and I wonder if Tess is actually feeding the whole festival or just family, friends, plus assorted hangers on. She cuts big hunks of wholemeal bread, one for each of us. There is home-made jam, Marmite, even butter in a small Tupperware box.

I'm seriously hungry. I've been up since before five, and it's near eleven now. Sleep-ins are compulsory at a festival, Tess tells me.

Leggit, who has been for a quick circuit of the camp, pausing only to wee on the grass outside Zak's tepee, trots up to Tess and collapses happily at her feet.

'Have you had her long?' I ask. 'Leggit?'

Finn shakes his head and rolls his eyes.

'Oh, no, Dizzy,' Tess is saying. 'Leggit's not *our* dog. No, she just comes scrounging around for leftovers. She's Storm's.'

The first signs of life are visible over at the tepee. The fiddle guy with the white beard crawls out through the doorflap, hauls himself up and stretches, groaning loudly. He picks up his fiddle-case and saunters off. Next, a large woman with long, grey plaits emerges, rubbing her eyes, trailing blankets.

I've eaten, downed two mugs of coffee and even managed a wash with warm water, soap and flannel in the privacy of Tess's tent by the time Storm and Zak appear, yawning, outside the tepee. I stare down at my bare feet, my toes threaded with grass and daisies while the waterlogged boots and socks dry out in the sun. I don't want to be like Mouse and Leggit, forgotten, sidelined. I don't want to be disappointed, even though I'm half expecting it.

But Storm shouts over straight away and I look up, grinning.

'Dizzy! Happy Solstice, babe!' she calls, picking her way barefoot across the grass. She swoops down, folding me up in a warm, patchouli-scented hug.

I know I can forgive her anything.

9

The festival slowly comes to life.

Zak and Finn and a gang of other blokes start moving logs and sticks and branches from the woodpile in the centre of the camp, hauling it up through the woods to the hilltop where the solstice bonfire will be.

All week, Storm says, they've been collecting firewood, picking up fallen branches from the woods, scrounging old pallets and broken packing cases. They have till tonight to build the biggest, tallest, best-ever bonfire on top of the hill.

'Should I help?' I ask, but Tess shakes her head and winks at me. She gives me a basket and asks me to unpack it in the clearing between the tents. I take out garden secateurs, string, glue, old yoghurt pots, sequins, paintbrushes, rusty scissors and a roll of masking tape.

I sit on the grass, baffled. Tess and Storm have gone. A dreadlocked woman with two little girls in neon T-shirts wanders up, smiling. She spreads a blanket on the grass and sits down. 'Gorgeous day,' she says lazily, and I agree. I try not to get worried when the kids start messing with the scissors and the sequins and the yoghurt pots.

The woman with the long, grey plaits appears, carrying a sheaf of coloured tissue paper. 'Want to sort it into different colours?' she asks the neon kids, and they do, making neat piles of soft, fluttery paper, weighting every pile with a stone.

'You're Storm's kid, Dizzy,' the grey-plaits woman says. 'Hi. My name is Amber. My partner's Carl, the guy with the fiddle, y'know? Ever do this before?'

Do what? Sit around in the afternoon sun with a couple of old hippies and a heap of rusty scissors?

'No, never,' I admit.

Two pink-haired women with grubby toddlers in tow amble over, then a thin, dark-skinned man wearing baggy trousers and a blue velvet waistcoat with no shirt underneath. By the time Tess and Storm turn up again, there are a dozen adults and almost as many kids sitting around on the grass.

Tess and Storm are carrying the bundles of long, skinny sticks I saw in the back of the patch-work van. Some are straight and strong, about as thick as my little finger, and some are thin and whippy.

'OK,' says Storm, hands on hips. 'We're going to make willow lanterns for the party. Here goes . . .'

I am now an expert in making willow lanterns. I have the glue-spattered cords and rainbow-stained fingers to prove it, because the dye in cheap tissue paper runs when it's wet.

First you make a pyramid shape with lengths of willow, binding the corners together with string and glue, then tear strips of coloured tissue to paste around the framework until it's covered.

Tess moves in and out of the crowd, leaning over to tighten a knot, pouring glue into yoghurt pots. She quietly rescues the wobbliest lanterns and gives them emergency first aid, until even the smallest toddler has something to be proud of.

Storm makes a lantern of dark blue and violet tissue paper, with a yellow crescent moon curving across one side. The other sides hold small, five-pointed stars filled with white tissue paper and dusted with silver glitter.

'Hey, Dizz, that's cool,' she says about my effort, a plain, lanky pyramid with random patches of red, purple and blue. It's not fancy, but it's OK for a first effort.

Storm helps the littlest kids, her fingers moving quickly, patching holes, replacing scrunched-up tissue, smoothing surfaces. 'You're a star,' she tells one small boy. Or, 'Wow, you must have done this before, yeah? What a natural.'

The children look up at her with shiny eyes, lapping up the praise. I bet I looked at her like that, once, before she went away.

No, actually. I bet I look at her like that *now*.

The grass sparkles with fallen sequins and grains of silver glitter, and eventually a whole crowd of multi-coloured lanterns sit on the grass beside the tepee, drying in the sun.

Tess gets stuck with the job of wiping small, sticky fingers and making endless herb teas for the adults. Storm and Amber put the candles in, a loop of wire hooks them on to a long carrying stick, and they're ready.

Like Storm says, cool.

Tess brings out a tin with a huge, dark, sticky cake in it. She cuts it into loads of pieces, so we all get a bit. It's carrot cake, and it's yummy.

'Is it vegan?' Storm asks, but doesn't wait for an answer. 'Mmm. I needed that.'

She sips herb tea the colour of washing-up water and rolls a ciggy. I look away so I don't have to know whether it's just tobacco or something else as well.

Zak and Mouse come up from the direction of the car-park field, carrying big, wide boxes hidden in bin bags.

'What's that, then?' Tess asks, but Zak just laughs.

'Wouldn't you like to know?' he says, and they march right on, into the woods above the camp, up the hill.

Finn appears with a couple of blokes in tow, hauling amps and speakers and a vast CD player up into the woods. The pink-haired women are making sandwiches from peanut butter and chocolate spread and mushroom pâté. Amber is making a cauldron of punch. I spot empty bottles of vodka and rum behind her tent.

'Loads of fruit,' she says, chopping up apples and oranges and limes. 'For energy. Want to do one for the kids?'

The neon sisters help me concoct a potion of cheap lemonade, Coke and apple juice. It tastes evil.

'Loads of sugar and E-numbers,' I tell Amber. 'For kids who want to stay up all night.'

Amber laughs.

Over by the tepee, Storm is setting out discs of paint, brushes, sponges, a mirror and a bowl of water. She calls over one of the neon sisters, picks up a brush, and paints a sunburst and rainbow on to her face. The other sister is transformed into a butterfly.

Soon, Storm has a queue of kids waiting to get their party faces.

'Come and help,' she calls over, and although I'm terrified and haven't a clue what I'm doing, I pick up a damp sponge and do what she tells me.

'White base, all over the face,' she says, nodding at the small boy at the head of the queue. 'Then a grey edging all round it, light, feathery strokes. A few grey smudges under the eyes and cheekbones. Kyle wants to be a vampire, right, kiddo?'

When I've got the base sorted, Storm moves in to do the fiddly bits and I move on to sponge yellow and orange all over a would-be tiger. I get better, faster. There's no time to be shy, and the kids aren't picky, anyway. They smile, they wriggle, they ask to be turned into cats and lions and witches and flowers.

'What a team,' Storm grins, setting loose her third butterfly of the afternoon. 'Way to go, Dizz, babe.'

We paint for hours, until just about every kid at the festival is bold and bright and beautiful. We charge a pound a face, 50p for arms and tattoos, free for anyone who knows Storm or anyone who hasn't got the cash on them right now. We make £3.50.

We stop for orange juice and Storm paints a curling, sweeping vine with soft, green leaves and tiny blue flowers spiralling round my arm. The brush tickles my wrist, then moves up to flicker softly across my face. When I glance in the cracked mirror, I see green lips, blue flower cheeks, emerald eyelashes spiralling out from around my eyes.

'My turn,' Storm says, presenting her thin, tanned face to be painted. I sponge it purple, adding swirls of pink and white, like the paisley-patterned quilts in the tepee.

The adults are stopping by now, some for a painted tattoo on a cheek or arm or shoulder blade, some for a full-face fantasy, a bird of paradise, a field of flowers, a summer sky.

I see Mouse watching from a distance, his pale face pinched and serious. I wave him over, but he blanks me.

Little girls start to appear with crowns made of willow, wildflowers and ribbon. Tess says they're selling them over by the other tepees, a quid a time. She's got one, a bright halo on her long, dark hair. I dive into the tepee and grab my camera so I can capture first Tess, then Storm.

People are spreading blankets and rugs across the centre clearing, bringing picnic baskets, cool boxes, carrier bags of food for the solstice picnic. A couple of blokes are selling lager, crisps, lemonade, bottled water, chocolate. Another slowly pushes a wheelbarrow laden with slabs of beer and bottles of cider up from the car park.

Tess has changed into a green velvet dress, and Storm appears in a white vest and pink crinkly trousers that billow down to her feet. When she moves, a million tiny bells jingle – she has soft cotton bands stitched with tiny silver bells tied round her ankles.

She scoops the face paints into a bag and heads off up the hill. She doesn't ask me to come. She leaves behind the cracked mirror, a gleam of silver in the yellowed grass. I pick it up.

The drumbeat is back, a low, steady pulse. The beardy guy, Carl, tunes up his fiddle. People sit down to eat and drink, because it's evening now, and the celebrations are about to begin.

The eldest neon sister, now a pink and blue butterfly in a pink embroidered dress, appears at my side.

'Shall I do your hair?'

She slips her hand into mine, and we sneak into the cool twilight of the tepee.

I change into clean jeans and a fresh T-shirt, taking care not to smudge the face paint. She unravels my plaits, spreading the hair out across my shoulders.

'My name's Cara,' she says as she brushes it smooth. 'I'm eight. How old are you?'

'Twelve,' I tell her.

'Can you sit on your hair?' she asks.

'Almost.'

She bites her lip and studies me seriously, like I'm her favourite Barbie doll. Then she pulls off her flowery crown and unknots two of the ribbons from the back, one red, one green. She combs out a slim hank of hair at the front, holds the red ribbon tightly at the top, and tells me to plait. I weave the ribbon in and out, making a long skinny plait, then do the same to the other side.

'I do this for my sister,' she says.

'You're very clever,' I tell her, and mean it. I pick up the cracked mirror and peer into it. I can hardly recognize myself beneath the swirls of face paint. Thick, mouse-brown waves fly out around my face. I will wear my hair loose more often. I look different, older, wilder.

I don't look scared any more.

By the time the picnic's over, it's almost dark. We trail up through the woods carrying lanterns, the drumbeat pounding and the fiddle singing squeakily as we crunch through the bracken and dead twigs. Cara and her little sister, Kai, hang on to my arm, dragging me forwards, pulling me back.

We leap the stream, and minutes later we're out of the woods again, on the hilltop.

'Wow!'

Huge rainbow flags and pennants flutter from tall poles, and a low boom of music floats down towards us from a cluster of rocks where someone has set up a generator, a CD player and a tiny stage made of planks and pallets. Two small dome-tents sit slantwise on the grass, looking like they're about to slide downwards. And on the hilltop stands the bonfire, a towering mound of logs and branches and boxes and splintered, smashed-up wood, silhouetted against the evening sky.

Suddenly the music dies and the drumbeat starts again, building slowly to a loud, thumping beat. A tall figure appears round the side of the hill, carrying three blazing sticks. His face and arms are painted with leaping flames, overlapping colours of red and orange and yellow. It's only because of his hair and his tattered jeans that I know it's Zak.

He lifts the three firebrands high and hurls one upwards, then all three are flying in perfect, swooping curves, through the air and down again to his waiting hands. I see Mouse watching, his eyes shining.

Zak juggles the firesticks higher and higher, on and on, until at last he throws one burning stick after another into the bonfire. As the flames lick gently around the scrunched-up newspaper and dry moss stuffed in among the wood, there's a huge bang behind us and the darkening sky explodes into millions of soft white stars.

'Fireworks!' shriek Cara and Kai, jumping up and down.

*That's* what was in the flat boxes Zak and Mouse were carrying.

There are rockets, fountains, screamers, even Catherine wheels tacked to the flagpoles. Someone's given sparklers to all the kids, and they write their names in the air, drawing zigzags, spirals, stars. The lanterns glow in stained-glass colours and the bonfire is blazing now, a roar and crackle of flames above us.

As the fireworks end, the music starts up again, and Storm swirls past me, a small, skinny whirlwind, grabbing my hand, dancing me round. Cara hangs on to my other hand, and everywhere now people are putting down their lanterns and joining on till there's a big line of people dancing, snaking round the hill, closer and closer to the big bonfire.

Carl runs along the line in the opposite direction, squealing his fiddle, raking the bow back and forth across the strings as his fingers fly. After him come the drummers, then a woman with a guitar, Zak juggling, Amber shaking a tambourine that trails ribbons.

I see a boy playing a tin whistle, his face painted with dozens of curling green leaves, dark, mossy, dreadlocked hair flopping forwards across blue-grey eyes.

Finn.

I dance until my breath is ragged, until we've circled the hill three times at least, until the line is breaking up and Cara and Kai and countless others have peeled away to find a drink, catch their breath, recover.

Those of us who are left drift up to the plank-and-pallet stage, where a CD player is belting out Oasis. For a while it's just Storm and me, our feet stamping a path round each other, our bodies arching, swerving, arms stretched out, fingers splayed, circling each other, laughing, gasping, dancing. Then Zak whirls in and grabs her hands and I back off, slow down and go in search of water.

It costs me a quid for what's meant to be fizzy spring water and turns out to be the warm, brackish stuff from the standpipe down at the camp. At least it's wet. I look for my lantern and find a different, abandoned one. I rescue it and sit down by the stage to watch Storm.

She's like a beautiful, exotic stranger. She's small, lean, brown, her shaven head thrown back as she dances, eyes closed now, lips parted, blissed out. The stud in her eyebrow glints in the light from a dozen tissue-paper lanterns. Her elbows jab and her arms flail as she twists and turns.

She's incredible, electric, unstoppable. Her energy could fuel this whole festival for a week.

The kids shimmy round her and beam when she touches their hair. The men watch her, too, their eyes held captive by her smile. Some of them dance near her, flirting, showing off, and she rewards them with a wink, a grin. Zak lets his hands skim over her face, staking his claim, but even he can't keep up with her. A few minutes later, he's picking up his juggling batons, heading back into the darkness, and Storm dances on.

She's my mum, although I'm not allowed to call her that, and I don't really know her, not yet. But I *will*.

Finn sits down beside me in the dark. 'Like it?' he asks, his face a dark shadow, forest green.

'*Love* it,' I say. 'It's unreal. I didn't know you played the tin whistle.'

Finn shrugs. 'I like music – and at a festival, anyone who plays anything gets roped in. You play guitar? I saw you carrying one yesterday.'

'I'm not very good yet,' I admit. 'I'm learning, at school.'

'Maybe I could show you a few chords.'

'OK, great. D'you play anything else?' I ask.

'Piano, a bit of flute,' Finn says. 'It's what I want to do, music. Go to music college, or start a band, or both.'

'*That's* what you're going to do when you're through with festivals.'

Finn laughs. 'I will,' he says. 'You just wait and see.'

I believe him.

'Your hair looks way better, loose,' he says, sipping a can of Coke.

'Your face looks way better, painted,' I retort.

'Watch it. I asked for that, I s'pose. It's just, you look older, y'know?'

'I know. You look – well, sort of *greener*. Like

you're . . .' I search for something clever to say. 'Branching out?'

'OK, OK,' he says. 'Enough. Let's just *leaf* it . . .'

'Ouch. Truce?'

'Truce,' he agrees.

We wander over to the giant bonfire, watching the flames leap upwards into the night. It's so hot, you can't stand too close, so we sit side by side on a fallen tree, cheeks burning, backs shivery.

'There's baked apples for later,' Finn says. 'You know, with raisins and honey where the core should be, all wrapped in foil. Tess put them in the embers earlier on, fifty or so of them.'

'I like your mum,' I say.

'I like *yours*.'

Before I can interrogate him on the subject of Storm, though, a small, pale-faced child moves round the bonfire in front of us. Mouse is staring into the flames, transfixed, his eyes huge, his mouth open.

He's far too close, but he doesn't seem to feel the heat. As we watch, he picks up a long, charred stick and prods it into the depths of the fire. The burning logs shift, crackling, the topmost branches collapse inwards and a blazing pallet crashes forwards, within inches of Mouse. A fresh wave of flames and sparks flare up, hissing.

'Mouse!'

Finn's on his feet in a second, pulling the stick from Mouse and throwing it into the fire.

'Mouse, that's not safe, pal,' he says, bending down. 'Fire's dangerous, you could hurt yourself. You have to treat it with respect.'

Mouse glares, his bottom lip jutting.

'You scared us, Mouse,' I chip in. 'Those burning branches could have fallen on *you*.'

He doesn't even look at me.

'Want a drink?' Finn asks gently, offering him his Coke. Mouse snatches the can and walks away.

'That kid has a problem,' I say to his retreating back.

'More than one,' Finn agrees.

I'm all partied out. I've danced so much my feet
are aching, even though the music is soppy and
ancient and sometimes seriously dodgy.

Finn gets to play the tin whistle some more,
up on the makeshift stage with Carl the beardy
guy, the guitar woman and the drummers. It isn't
exactly a band, and it's a million miles from being
cool, but it's fun and it's loud and everyone is
dancing or watching or singing along.

Later, Finn borrows the guitar and sits on the
edge of the stage to sing a few songs I don't recognize. Nobody pays much attention, just me and
Tess and a couple of blitzed-looking crusties. I see
Mouse, sitting to one side of the stage, his arms
round Leggit, his little face pale and intense in the
moonlight, watching, listening.

When I look round again, he's gone.

Further up the hillside, a few bodies lie flat out
on the grass, staring at the sky or snoring loudly

where they've fallen. The music gets slower, softer. The dancing stops. Tess sits by the stage with a blanket wrapped round her, telling bedtime stories to a knot of kids too stubborn or too stoked up on the E-number punch to give in to exhaustion.

Storm sits by the bonfire, watching the stars. She points out the Great Bear and the Little Bear, telling me how the Roman god Jupiter made them when he bewitched a beautiful woman and her son and threw them up into the sky.

'See those bright stars along the tail of the Great Bear,' Storm says softly, 'like a saucepan with a crooked handle? That's the Big Dipper. If you line up the two stars at the end of the Dipper, they point to a big, bright star at the tip of the Little Bear's tail. That's the Pole Star, the most magical star in the sky. You can always see it, anywhere you are in the northern hemisphere. I've seen it in Nepal, and in Morocco. Wherever you are, Dizz, make time to look at the stars.'

'They don't have stars in Birmingham,' I tell her. 'The sky's all orange from all the millions of streetlamps. You can't see anything else.'

Storm ruffles my hair. 'Hey, the Pole Star is *always* there,' she says. 'Even in Birmingham. Even if you can't see it. Might be too bright from the streetlamps, might be too cloudy, but that star is always there. Remember that.'

'I will.'

When the sun finally comes up, it's like someone's spread a bright tie-dye quilt all over the valley below us. The sky is streaked with pink and mauve and soft, pale yellow, and then the sun appears, a big circle of shimmering pink and gold.

'That's it, then, for another year,' Finn says. 'You tired?'

'Mmm,' I say dreamily, but I've gone past tired, past hungry, past everything. My eyes are wide open, gritty, aching. My bare feet are stained green and brown from the grass and mud, because I took my trainers off hours ago to dance, and now I can't find them.

I look at Finn, his face-paint streaked into a mess of smears.

'Your leaves are falling,' I tell him.

'You can talk,' he counters. 'You look like you've had a fight with an extra-large pizza.'

'I wish!'

We mooch around the hillside, looking for my trainers. I find one stranded in the middle of the grass and one, slightly singed, at the edge of the smouldering bonfire.

A convoy of hippy blokes head off down the hillside with the amps, speakers and generator. Clumps of people head back down to the camp, trailing tattered lanterns.

Finn and I wander downhill, picking our way around the diehard revellers who just can't leave. Carl is still playing the fiddle, a mournful salute to the rising sun. Halfway down the hill, Storm and Zak sit sharing a ciggy, squinting into the distance, holding hands.

'Dizzy, babe,' says Storm sleepily as we go past.

I turn back on impulse and duck down to plant a quick kiss on her neck. My mum, human whirl-wind, dancing queen, total party animal.

Her face-paint tattoos are streaked and smudgy, and there are wrinkles around her eyes, across her forehead. She looks small and tired and vulner-able, but the stud in her eyebrow gleams golden and proud.

Down by the dome-tents, Cara's mum is trying to shake her awake.

'Want a piggy-back?' Finn asks gently, and Cara nods, bleary-eyed. He squats down and Cara climbs on, arms hooking tightly round Finn's neck. We go slowly through the woods, splash across the stream. I take a detour to peer into the little den, and there's Mouse, collapsed on top of his sleeping bag, Leggit's hairy face snuffled into his neck.

We reach the camp and Finn finds a last burst of energy from somewhere, galloping down through the trees, leaping guy-ropes and racing around the tents whooping while Cara screeches with delight.

A crusty bloke with bloodshot eyes crawls out of a tent and lets loose a torrent of swear words. Finn skids to a halt in front of him, dropping a deep bow and letting Cara slip gently to the ground.

'Idiot,' Tess says, affectionately. 'People are trying to sleep.'

'But it's morning! Time to get up, get moving, get happy!'

'No,' says Tess firmly. 'Time to wash, eat and go to bed. Don't argue.'

Cara wanders off to find her mum, and Finn and I flop down next to Tess. There's a bowl of warm, soapy water and a flannel, and I wash my face as best I can. Tess takes the flannel and wipes the bits I've missed, then scrubs at Finn's face like he's six years old. He grins at me, brown and shiny and dripping wet.

Tess makes mugs of hot apple juice. We scoff down muesli and chopped bananas, and then I'm yawning, fading fast. I say goodnight to Tess and Finn and drift over to the tepee.

I pause for a moment in the doorway, looking out across the camp. The multi-coloured tents are sleeping now, and it's quiet except for a distant drumbeat and the sound of a dog barking, up in the woods.

The morning light is thin and pink and dappled, like the world is all brand new.

I sleep all day, wake up in time for a bowlful of Tess's vegetable soup, and then sleep again. Staying up all night is pretty exhausting. The camp is full of sleepy, lazy people, smiling, smoking, trying to recover.

The day after, Finn and I scour the hillside around the embers of the solstice bonfire, filling bin bags with cans and bottles and rubbish. The bottles go into one bag, the cans into another, the rubbish into a couple more. We find dead fireworks, lost ribbons, sweet wrappers, cigarette stubs, smashed willow lanterns, scorched jam jars.

'Why are we *doing* this?' I ask, binning yet another sticky paper cup.

'For the Earth,' Finn reminds me. 'For the animals, the trees. And because the farmer gave us a fiver to get it cleared.'

'We've been ripped off,' I tell him.

Finn stuffs one final bag with lost property. Two

watches, a blue jumper, a pair of black lace-up boots, size ten, a purple suede jacket, a silver bracelet, five plastic cigarette lighters, a squashed mobile phone, a child's cardigan, a spotty scarf, a wallet with seventeen pounds and twenty-four pence plus a cashpoint card inside.

'What'll we do with it all?'

'The lost stuff, we spread it all out on a blanket back at the camp for people to claim,' Finn explains. 'If it's something valuable, they'll maybe give us 50p to say thanks. I'll sell the lighters on for 10p a go . . .'

'You're selling people back the stuff they lost the night before last?'

'Sure.' Finn shrugs. 'If they were *that* bothered, they'd have gone back up yesterday to look. We're providing a service, aren't we?'

We leave the lost-property bag in Tess's tent. We drag the rubbish, tins and bottles down through the copse of hazels and past the car-park field. We haul the rubbish bags along a farm-track and leave them knotted by the farmer's big wheelie bins, then set off to the village with the sacks of bottles and cans because Tess says there are recycling skips just behind the primary school. She's given us some cash and a shopping list, too, so we can get some supplies in the village shop.

It's a long walk, especially with heavy, clanking

bin bags. When we get to the village, a few locals give us funny looks, and I try hard not to care, because I'm with Finn and he clearly doesn't.

We find the bottle bank and drop bottles through the holes marked 'clear', 'brown' and 'green', and listen to them smash and clink. Then we stuff squished-up cans into the can bank.

Finn wipes his hands on his tattered jeans. 'Shopping, next,' he grins.

There is a post office and a general store in the village. When we go into the post office so I can choose a postcard for Dad, everyone goes quiet and watches us. I pick a pretty mountain view and pay for it quickly, pink-faced.

'Why are they so . . . funny?' I ask Finn, when we get outside again. 'It's like they've never seen kids before.'

'Probably haven't,' Finn says. 'Not crusty kids, anyhow. There's never been a festival here before, and people get all stressy and think you're going to start nicking things and pushing drugs to the local toddlers. Take no notice.'

'But I'm not . . . a *crusty* kid,' I protest.

Finn looks at me, his grey eyes laughing. 'No?' he says. 'What are you, then?'

I bite my lip.

I'm wearing yesterday's T-shirt with a big, brown stain down one side from a beer can that dripped when I was recycling it. My jeans are dusty with bonfire ash, and there's a sticky bit on one leg where I dropped my bread and honey earlier. My new plum trainers are black with mud and dust and grass-stains. I brushed my hair this morning, but there's a breeze today and I know it's all frizzy and wild, the way it gets when I don't plait it. And, worst of all, after breakfast, I allowed Cara to draw a flower on my cheek with her felt-tipped pens. I never even checked it in the mirror.

'I'm just me,' I say sadly. 'I'm Dizzy.'

'OK,' shrugs Finn. 'That's good enough for me.'

Inside the general store he dredges out Tess's shopping list and starts piling up a basket with white bread and milk and cheese and pasta. I drift off into the next aisle looking for teabags, then stop short. Ahead of me at the till is Mouse, with Leggit behind him sniffing around in the fruit and veg.

'Don't let your dog touch the veg, pet, it's not hygienic,' the woman at the till is saying, as Mouse puts a can of Coke, a box of matches and a handful of penny sweets up on to the counter.

'You don't have enough money,' she frowns, scrabbling through the change in his palm. 'You'll have to put the Coke back. How about one of these instead? They're cheaper.'

She turns away to reach down a small plastic bottle of fizzy pop.

I'm about to call out and tell Mouse we'll treat him when I see his hands dart out, stuffing chocolate bars into his trouser pockets, scooping up the sweets and matches. The woman turns back just in time to see him fly out of the shop like a small tornado, Leggit at his heels.

My jaw drops open, horrified.

'Stop!' yells the shop assistant. 'I *saw* that! Come back!'

She looks like she's about to sprint off down the street after him, but then she spots me and Finn and her mouth sets into a hard, furious line.

'Is he with you?' she demands. 'You saw that, didn't you? He nicked a load of chocolate! Bloody travellers. Everyone said this festival would be nothing but trouble.'

Finn marches down the aisle and dumps his basket on the counter.

'He's not with us, no. In fact, I never saw him before in my life. But I'll pay you for the stuff anyway – will two quid cover it, d'you think?'

The woman rings up our shopping with a face like thunder. She takes Finn's money, including enough to cover what Mouse nicked. Finn peels off a couple of plastic carriers and we pack the shopping in silence.

'Running wild,' she mutters. 'Where's the parents, that's what I'd like to know? Drunk, I bet

– or worse. You try to be nice, but what do you get? Thieving kids and scabby dogs slavering all over the fruit and vegetables. Shouldn't even *be* in the shop. It's disgusting.'

'Want me to pay for that, too?' Finn asks, pleasantly.

'Hmphh. Suppose not. Just tell them people up at the festival to keep that kid away from here, OK?'

'No problem,' Finn beams. 'Have a nice day, now!'

The door swings shut behind us. The village street is still bright and sunny, the cottages still postcard-perfect, but it feels cold and hard and unfriendly now.

'That was awful.' My voice sounds all thin and wobbly. 'That woman was *horrible*. How did you manage to stay so polite?'

'Part of the training,' Finn shrugs. 'People judge you when you're a traveller. They think you're dirty, they think you're scum. I used to get upset and angry, but Tess taught me that staying cool is the best way to handle it. Show them that you're as good as anyone.'

'I know, but Mouse . . .'

'Stupid kid,' Finn says. 'If he's going to nick stuff, he could at least try not to be seen.'

'*If* he's going to nick stuff . . .?'

84

My head is reeling.

'OK,' Finn says. 'It's wrong, I know, but Mouse is a pretty messed-up kid. He steals. It's a fact. He'll not stop just because I ask him to.'

'Do Storm and Zak know?'

'Course they know,' Finn laughs. 'Everyone knows.'

'Oh.'

We're nearly out of the village now. An old man stops digging his vegetable patch to give us a long, icy stare, and Finn retaliates with a cheery wave, flicking back his dreadlocks for effect.

'Don't you hate it, though?' I ask. 'People staring, people thinking you're dirt?'

'I used to hate it, yeah. But now it doesn't seem to matter so much. *I* know who I am, where I'm going. That's what matters. If someone chooses to think I'm rubbish just because I've got funny hair and scruffy clothes – well, so what? They don't even know me, do they?'

'No, I suppose not.'

We walk back along the lanes, swinging the shopping bags. I try to imagine what it's like to be a full-time crusty kid, with tangly hair, dirty fingernails, raggedy jeans. I try to imagine a whole lifetime of being frowned at by shopkeepers, teachers, silver-haired grannies.

'You can't really blame them, thinking the

worst,' Finn adds. 'It's because they're scared. They really do think we're all no-good, thieving, drugged-up hippies.'

'But it's not *like* that.'

Finn gives me a long, hard look.

'OK, it *is* like that. But it's not *horrible*. Is it?'

'You asking me, or yourself?' Finn laughs. 'Mouse better hope word doesn't get back to Zak about this. The poor kid has had enough upsets. He's missing his mum, he doesn't want to be here in the first place . . . Tess reckons the stealing thing is a cry for help.'

'He's trying to get some attention,' I suggest.

'Yeah, only the kind of attention Zak's likely to give won't exactly help. He scared him half to death last time.'

We walk for a while in silence, while I take this in.

'What happened to Mouse's mum?' I ask then. 'Is she ill or something?'

'Something,' says Finn, shortly.

'You mean she just left him, like – like Storm left me?' I blurt out.

Only worse, I think, because Mouse didn't have a dad around to bail him out. Instead, he got carted halfway across the country to stay with a dad he probably couldn't even remember and a stepmum he'd never met.

Tough deal.

'His mum didn't *want* to leave him,' Finn says carefully. 'She couldn't help it. She's got . . . big problems. She can't really look after herself, let alone him.'

'But why?'

Finn kicks up a cloud of dust and gravel as we turn off the lane and on to the steep farm-track.

'I suppose you might as well know. Mouse is here because his mum is a junkie, OK? A heroin addict, a smackhead. And right now she's in rehab, in London, trying to get clean.'

I stare at Finn, my eyes wide, my mouth dry.

What do you say to that?

Dear Dad,
I've been at the festival for five days now, and it's brilliant! We're sleeping in a tepee, which is weird – I think I prefer my bed at home. On Tuesday we're moving on to another festival, and Storm says you might be meeting us there. I can't wait to see you. I'm missing you loads. See you soon.
  Love,
    Dizzy xxxxxxx

'What's that, then, Dizz?' Storm asks as I put down my pen.

'It's a postcard for Dad.' I scan quickly over the lines, trying to decide if Storm will mind that I've put I'm not crazy about the tepee, or that I'm missing Dad. I decide she won't.

'Can I see?'

I hand the postcard over and she reads it quickly, eyes narrowed.

'I'll post it later,' I say lightly. 'I forgot to get a stamp.'

The people in the post office were so icy I only just managed to pay for the postcard without getting frostbite, so going back for stamps is not something I'm looking forward to.

'Want me to do it, babe?' Storm says. 'I'm going down to the village anyway. Zak's doing a crystal-healing session on Jim Dean and he needs peace and quiet. Keep Mouse away from the tepee, won't you, Dizz?'

'No problem. And thanks, Storm.'

Crystal healing is Zak's thing. I know he takes it seriously because nobody's allowed near the little wooden box where he keeps his crystals, and no-body's allowed near the tepee when he's working.

Crystal healing is an art, Storm says. Zak's little chunks of crystal are full of earth energies, and Zak's healing hands help to channel the energy and create deep, healing powers. It also costs twenty pounds a go, so Jim Dean, who looks like a sleepy skeleton with long hair and a beard, must take it seriously too.

'He's got gout,' Finn whispers. 'Every time he drinks too much, his foot hurts like crazy.'

'Can Zak *cure* that?' I ask, eyes wide.

'Doubt it,' Finn grins. 'But Jim'll have less cash to spend on booze.'

I stifle a giggle, and Storm turns back to look at me, frowning.

'Tell you what,' she says. 'Any other postcards you want to send to Pete, just give them to me and I'll get them posted. I can add my own messages on the end, say hi, y'know?'

'OK. Thanks, Storm. But I'll be seeing Dad soon, anyway, won't I?'

'Sure,' she says, with a slow, easy grin. 'Sure you will, babe. *Soon*.'


When Storm gets back from the village later, all hell breaks loose. I have never seen her angry before.

She marches through the campsite, her face pale with fury. She chucks her rucksack on the grass and shoves Tess out of the way rudely when she tries to remind her about Zak's crystal-healing session.

I put down my guitar, jump to my feet. 'Storm? Mum? What's wrong?'

Storm ignores me and heads straight for the tepee, dragging up the doorflap and hooking it to one side. 'Zak!' she bellows. 'He's done it again. The little git has done it again.'

Tess, Finn and I rush over to the tepee and catch sight of Jim Dean, wearing nothing but a pair of orange boxer shorts, lying flat out in the middle of the floor. A line of little crystals is balanced all along his spine, and Zak's healing hands hover mysteriously above his head.

'Storm,' says Zak tightly, 'not now. Whatever it is, it can wait. I'm in the middle of a *healing* . . .'

'It – can – *not* – wait,' snaps Storm.

Zak's hands drop down to his sides, and Jim Dean leaps up, wrapping himself in a tie-dye sarong. Crystals scatter as he moves, all over the floor.

'Just about done, anyway,' he says, grabbing his T-shirt and limping past us out of the tepee.

'So . . .?'

'It's Mouse, isn't it?' Storm explodes. 'He's only gone and nicked a kid's scooter from the village. He's already been barred from both the shops for stealing stuff – apparently, he was away with a tenner's worth of chocolate, yesterday.

'What's wrong with him? Can't you control him? Can't you *do* something? If he shows his face in that village again, they'll have him strung up!'

'Trouble,' Finn whispers. 'Big trouble. I'll go look for Mouse. Maybe we can get that scooter back to the village before things get any worse.'

He slips quietly away. Tess puts a hand on my sleeve, and together we take a few steps backwards.

Zak looks flushed and angry.

'How d'you know it's him nicked the scooter?' he's saying.

'How many seven-year-old thieves d'you think we've got up here?' Storm roars. 'Come on, Zak, wake up. Small, skinny, filthy kid with matted brown hair and a big black-and-white dog at his heels. Who else is it going to be?'

'He's had a tough time,' Zak says lamely.

'He'll have a tougher one, soon, if I get my hands on him,' Storm snaps. 'If you don't get him sorted out soon those villagers will have the police up here. We're lucky they haven't already.' She stares at Zak for a long moment, her eyes blazing, then she seems to slump, her anger gone.

Tess takes my hand and leads me out of the tepee, letting the doorflap drop behind us. 'Don't worry, love,' she whispers. 'It'll blow over. She lives up to her name, sometimes, that's all.'

'What about Mouse?' I ask, my voice shaky.

'Little idiot,' Tess says, softly. 'We'd better find him, quick, before Zak does.'

Mouse is in big trouble.

OK, that's nothing new. Trouble and Mouse go hand in hand. He's a thief. His mum is a drug addict. His dad ignores him.

That suits Mouse. It's safer being invisible, only today he's not quite invisible enough, and Finn finally tracks him down. He hides out in Tess's tent eating cake and slurping apple juice, while Finn and I trek down to the village with the stolen scooter.

Finn looks straight ahead, wheeling the scooter right down the centre of the main street. He doesn't flinch when a couple of kids point and laugh at him, or when a knot of women outside the post office break off from their gossip to stare, stony-faced. I do, though. My cheeks flush crimson and I try to hide behind my hair. We leave the scooter outside the shop, because we don't know who it belongs to and there's no way we can ask.

'We found it,' Finn says to the silent street. 'And we've brought it back. OK?'

The hard-faced women shake their heads in disgust, and a small boy blows a loud, squelchy raspberry before bolting for safety.

Finn goes into the shop and buys a couple of Cokes, while I hover behind him, terrified. When we come out again, the street is deserted and the scooter is gone.

'Bloody Mouse,' says Finn, tearing at his ring-pull.

'He didn't mean it,' I whisper, although I think he probably did. 'At least you brought it back. They're bound to be mad at us, aren't they, the villagers?'

'Just a bit.'

Back at the festival, the music has stopped, the mood's gone flat. A few people are packing up, talking about moving on.

Zak is shouting at Mouse. You cannot have a row in a tepee without half the campsite hearing it.

'Even Mouse couldn't hide forever,' Finn says.

Storm and Tess are sitting in the last dregs of sunshine, sipping herb tea and looking sad. 'Zak gets so cross,' Storm says helplessly. 'Poor little Mouse.'

I wonder if she's somehow forgotten that she got cross first, that *she* got Zak all wound up. I wonder if she's forgotten all the awful things she called Mouse.

Maybe.

'C'mon, Dizzy, babe,' she says then, flinging an arm round my shoulder. 'Let's go cool things down, yeah?'

'Dizzy can stay here,' Tess says. 'No hassle.'

'No, Tess,' Storm says firmly. 'Thanks, but this is a family problem, y'know? We're all in it together.'

I blink, remembering a whole raft of family problems Dad and I had to sort alone, while Storm was hanging out with her hippy mates in Kathmandu and Marrakesh. We weren't all in it together then.

But this is a *different* family, of course. Maybe Storm values it more.

Tess and Finn shoot me a sympathetic look, but nobody argues. Even I get the message that there's just no point. Storm sweeps across to the tepee and propels me inside. Zak stops, mid-rant, and glares at us, then drops his gaze to Mouse.

'Oh, I give up,' he says heavily. 'You're a no-good, lying, thieving little toe-rag and I'm sick of the sight of you.'

Mouse tries to look defiant, but a huge tear rolls down his grimy cheek. His lip quivers.

'Zak, what chance has he had to learn right

from wrong?' Storm argues. 'Poor little mite, he never had a hope. We can help him forget the past, learn new ways.'

'How can we help him when he's never here?' Zak bursts out. 'The kid's half wild, isn't he? Well, you stay around *me* from now on, Mouse. You do as you're told. You eat here, sleep here, help out. Is that clear?'

Mouse nods, mutely.

'Dizzy, you'll look out for him, won't you, babe?' Storm says. 'Keep him right, check he's in at night, keep him out of trouble? Keep him out of our hair?'

I swallow. This sounds like a full-time job, with overtime.

'Well, you might as well do *something* to earn your keep,' Zak snarls. 'What are we, a bloody orphanage? A holiday camp?'

I freeze. Zak glowers at me, and suddenly I suss that as far as he's concerned, I'm about as welcome here as an outbreak of the plague.

'Zak, honey,' Storm says sweetly, stroking his cheek, his hair. 'Dizzy's a *good* girl. She'll keep an eye on Mouse. And I can claim money for looking after her. We'll be one big, happy family.'

Zak laughs out loud, but there's no warmth in his laugh. I decide that I don't like him, not one little bit.

'It's not for long,' I say in a small voice. 'Dad's coming next week, isn't he? I could always ring him now and explain . . .'

'Nah, don't bother,' Zak says coldly. 'He'll come and get you, won't he? Or maybe he'll join the big, happy family, too. The more the merrier, eh, Storm?'

Mouse edges closer to me. He's still scowling, his brow knotted, but he slips his hand into mine. It feels small and light, like you could snap the bones with a single squeeze.

'Your dad'll be here next week or the week after,' Storm says to me. 'No need to ring him, worry him. We *want* you here, don't we, Zak? We need you here. Don't run out on us just yet, please, babe?'

Zak sits down against a bank of velvet cushions, and the anger seems to drain away from him. Storm stays close, smoothing his hair.

'Look, I didn't mean to shout, Dizzy,' Zak says. 'It's just been a well-stressful day, yeah? Storm's right, we need you. Just help us get Mouse back on track, OK? Stay another week or two. More if you like. Really.'

I nod, feeling numb.

'It's OK,' Storm says softly. 'It's OK. We can be a family.'

Mouse looks at me, his eyes wide. For the first

time since I came here, I begin to understand. He's like me, Mouse. He never had a family, not a proper one. Not the mum, dad and 2.4 children kind. It's like we both got given a jigsaw with half the bits missing, and had to make a picture anyway.

His mum let him down, big-style, just like Storm did me. We may not like each other, Mouse and I. Not yet. But we both know that playing at families is not a game.

Storm scrapes stale breadcrusts with the last of the peanut butter, and we sit together round the tepee fire and eat. It tastes awful and it's not even filling, but we're not about to complain. Zak and Storm sit up smoking and talking, and in the distance I can hear Finn playing the penny whistle and, later, an owl hooting in the darkness.

When I'm woken by Mouse's whimpering cries, I know it's very, very late. I struggle up on to my elbows, peering out across the tepee.

'Not again! Can't you shut him up?' Zak growls.

Leggit barks raggedly, then subsides to a whine.

'For God's *sake*!'

I reach out into the darkness and touch the rough blanket Mouse has rolled around himself. I shake him gently. 'Mouse, wake up!' I hiss.

There's a long shudder, and the whimpering stops.

'It's OK,' I whisper. 'Just a nightmare.'

Mouse squirms, crawling closer in the dark. I let my arm fall round him, pulling him near. Leggit snuffles round and curls against his shoulder, her raggedy tail tickling my face.

Mouse smells of chocolate and peanut butter and fear. Sometimes, in the dark, I hear him sniff. I don't have to touch his face to know it's damp with tears.

Mouse is scared. I know it, I feel it and I understand.

I'm scared too.

15

We spend all day taking down the tent and the tepee, packing stuff away, rolling canvas, carefully lowering the huge larch poles and lashing them on to the roof rack of the patchwork van. The festival field looks sad and scruffy, covered in yellow and brown blotches where tents and tepees once were. There are only a handful of tents left, a few stragglers too lazy or too chilled to pack up and go.

Storm asks Tess to drive Mouse and Leggit and me to the next festival. Zak's going to drive the patchwork van at night, so it'll be less noticeable, less likely to be stopped by police. He ties a huge tie-dye rag on to the jutting larch poles, just to make sure the van definitely qualifies as Weirdest Vehicle in the Entire Universe. If I was a police patrol, *I* wouldn't stop it. I'd report it to the FBI as an alien spaceship.

Everyone hugs, and Storm asks Tess to save them a good space at the Tree People Festival. Tess promises. Then the first big drops of rain start falling, and we sprint for the car. Storm and Zak stand in the car-park field getting soaked to the skin, waving. Then the car judders round a bend in the track and they're gone.

The wipers swish across the windscreen and Tess peers out over the road, frowning, scooshing through puddles and swerving to avoid the occasional frog. Finn is in the front seat, fighting with a fold-out map that's threatening to take over the whole car. Mouse and Leggit and I are squashed in the back, bags and bedding wedged in around us.

After a while, we stop in a grey, drizzly town to invade the launderette. Tess hauls out bin bags of dirty washing and we pack four machines to bursting point. It's not just Tess and Finn's stuff – I spot Zak's tie-dye shirts, Storm's stripy trousers, a few mud-caked T-shirts that have to belong to Mouse, and loads of my jeans and tops and undies. Clean clothes!

Tess winks at me, pours in washing powder, sets the machines and checks her watch. 'Shopping,' she says. 'OK?'

We find a supermarket and Tess fills a trolley to overflowing, not just bread and rice and cheese and beans, but hot chocolate and fresh pineapple and strawberries and cheesecake and Hi-Juice apple squash. Then we go back to the launderette to drag the washing into the driers.

I bought a postcard in the supermarket, so I scribble a quick message while we wait.

Dear Dad,
I'm writing this in a launderette in the Scottish borders – never thought I'd miss our washing machine or the iron, but I do! We'll be at the Tree People Festival by nightfall. Storm says you'll be joining us there soon – I can't wait! Missing you like mad,

Dizzy xxxx
PS Tess, Finn and Mouse say hi. And Leggit the lurcher!

Tess offers to post the card, but I remember what Storm said and stick it in my pocket to show her first. She might want to add a few directions to the festival for Dad.

By the time we've folded the clean, dry clothes, packed them back into bin bags and stuffed them into an already bulging car, everyone's starving. It's way past teatime. We head for the chippy, because Tess says we deserve it, and anyway, she won't want to be bothered cooking once we get to the Tree People place.

Tess and Finn have fish 'n' chips, I have curry

and chips and Mouse has chips with fish, potato scallops, a battered sausage, a mini pizza, a pineapple fritter, beans, bread rolls and every kind of ketchup. His hand sneaks out to nick a Twix while the assistant's back is turned, but Tess slaps his knuckles sharply.

'I'd have bought it for you if you'd asked,' she says briskly. 'Too bad. You don't steal while you're with us, Mouse. You just have to *ask*. We don't rip each other off, and we don't rip off others either. Got it?'

Mouse nods, staring at his boots.

'Sorry,' he mumbles after a minute, and Tess grins like she's just won the Lotto, then ruffles his hair.

We dodge through the rain and pile back into the car, where Leggit waits on the driver's seat with her head out of the partly open window, dripping wet. When we get in, she ricochets around the car with delight, snuffling at our faces, sitting on our chips.

Tess heads out of the town and on along the little, twisty lanes. The car reeks of vinegar and curry sauce. Mouse gives the battered sausage to Leggit, plus a good quarter of his chips. He wraps the leftovers carefully and stashes them away for later.

Finn drips tomato ketchup all over the map,

Leggit puts a paw through the centre of East Kilbride and Mouse falls asleep, his head against my shoulder. We drive on through the rain.

It's almost dark by the time we arrive. We drive under a vast white banner that says 'Tree People Festival' in fancy letters, on to a huge field dotted sparsely with tents and edged with a fast-running river. We're early, Tess says. The festival doesn't start properly until the weekend.

Our headlamps rake across Amber, trailing across the field in an orange cagoule and a pointy Peruvian hat, carrying water. She tells us she's camped down by the river with Carl, the neon twins and their mum and a whole raft of others I've never even heard of. Tess parks up a little way back from the semi-circle of tents, headlights blazing.

Pitching a tent at night in the pouring rain is no joke. Amber and Tess wrestle with the inner tent while Finn slots together the curving framework. Mouse and I hang on to the flapping corners of the waterproof shell, while the others hammer in tent-pegs, trip over guy-ropes and tug at knots. The rain streams down my face and drips inside my collar.

By the time I've hauled the bedding from car to tent, I'm drenched to the skin. Finn and Mouse are off walking Leggit and checking out the toilet block, which is rumoured to have a hot shower. Tess throws me a towel and tells me to get changed and into my sleeping bag. I do as she says, feeling soggy, exhausted, too tired to care.

Mouse and Leggit explode into the tent, dripping. Leggit shakes herself all over me, then stretches out, making a wet patch on my sleeping bag. Mouse shrugs off his anorak and rolls a quilt round himself, fully dressed. His hair is plastered flat against his head, and I dry it gently with the towel.

Finn arrives with water and Tess fires up the Calor gas, handing out mugs of hot apple juice. We sip our drinks by torchlight, except for Mouse, who's asleep already.

It's more of a sardine can than a four-man tent, but we're so tired nobody cares. I wake briefly, deep in the night, to the low, rumbling rattle of what has to be the patchwork van and the bright sweep of its headlights. Then the engine stutters into silence and the headlamps die, and although I listen out hard for Storm and Zak, there's only silence in the dark blue night. I roll over and sleep.

The rumours are true. There *are* showers in the Portakabin toilet block. I beg 10p pieces from Tess and stand under the hot streams of water to wash away a week of grime. The water runs grey as I scrub at the shadows of Cara's latest felt-pen tattoos, shampoo my hair twice and slather on conditioner. Every few minutes the water fizzles out, but I feed more money into the slot until someone banging on the shower door drags me down from heaven.

Outside the Portakabin, Finn is waiting, his own hair damp from the men's shower, his feet bare on the rain-wet grass. 'Thought you'd washed yourself away,' he grins. 'So *that's* what you look like, clean. I'd just about forgotten.'

I flick him with my towel and he runs away, dodging through the tents and cars and battered-looking vans that are scattered across the site. Some of them make the patchwork van look almost smart. Almost, but not quite.

There's no sign of life inside Storm and Zak's van, but Tess is up, setting out cereal and strawberries and milk. Mouse, who prefers a healthy breakfast, is halfway through the chocolate spread, and Leggit has snaffled last night's leftover chips, including the paper.

'I like it here,' I announce.

'Because?' Finn prompts.

'It's beautiful,' I say. 'The river, the trees, the mountains in the distance. But mainly it's because we've got hot showers, bin bags full of clean clothes and loads of food. Plus, I know some of the people this time. I'm getting the hang of it, y'know? And Dad's coming soon!'

'Not that you're sick of us or anything!' Finn laughs.

'No way! But Dad'll stick around for a bit, maybe. That's what Storm says.'

'I didn't know your dad was coming,' Tess says. 'It's *years* since I've seen Pete. When's he due, then?'

'I don't know,' I admit. 'But he's definitely coming, Storm said. Soon.'

'Right. Funny she never mentioned it – I thought it was just you. Still, it'll be great to see Pete. Like old times!'

Tess attacks the chocolate smeared around Mouse's face with a wet flannel, managing to clear some of it before he ducks away.

I'll have to pin down Storm about exactly when Dad's coming. I'll have to make sure he knows where we are, and how to get here. I know he's going to love it, seeing old friends like Tess and Finn, meeting Mouse and Leggit and Zak. Well, maybe not Zak.

I hope Dad comes soon. I miss him like mad.

Dear Dad,

There's loads going on here! I've done workshops in paper-making and felt-making and drumming! I've eaten falafel in pitta bread and deep-fried tofu fritters and sushi rolls with sour pickled vegetables and seaweed. I've had my hands painted with henna, helped to carve a giant totem pole and learnt to weave friendship bracelets. Come soon or you'll miss all the fun!

         Big hugs,

             Dizzy xxxx

It's a great festival.

There are stalls selling hats from Nepal, itchy jumpers from Peru, tin mirrors from Tunisia. You can buy wind chimes made of seashells and bracelets made from old silver forks, the prongs curled round in little spirals. There's soap made from dandelions and shampoo brewed from boiled-up twigs.

Everyone's doing *something*.

Storm puts a sign on the patchwork van, advertising tarot readings. A steady stream of hippies drift by each day and part with cash to hear her tell the future. She tells them about tall, dark strangers, travel overseas, a new baby, a new career, a dream come true. One day, I hear her telling Amber that she's at a crossroads in her life, that she'll take the path that's least expected.

'The tarot never lie,' she tells Amber.

I frown, trying to remember the things she told me.

'Can Storm see into the future?' I ask Tess later. 'Is it real, the stuff she says? Do the tarot ever lie?'

Tess laughs.

'The tarot's a great way to make money,' she says. 'Everyone wants to know the future. Will we be happy or sad, rich or poor, loved or lonely? I don't know, pet, I'm the wrong person to ask. I gave up on fairy-tale endings a long time ago. You have to make your own luck in this life.'

'Does *Storm* believe it?' I ask.

Tess shrugs. 'Hard to tell, with Storm. Mostly, she tells you what you want to hear. She doesn't mean any harm – it's just the way she is.'

'Just a way to make money,' I repeat.

'Pretty much,' Tess says.

Did Storm really see adventure and travel in my

cards, or did she just say it because it suited her plans? I have to trust her, don't I? Like Amber does, and all the others who queue up to part from their fivers in return for a little bit of future.

Anyone foolish enough to hand over their cash to Zak, however, deserves everything they get – and what they get, in my opinion, is fleeced. The tepee is out of bounds between midday and four each day, when Zak has his crystal-healing sessions. Big deal. I mean, it's not like we'd want to watch, is it?

Every night there's music and dancing and drinking. Every night the tepee is crammed with crusties, thick with smoke, awash with cider.

Mouse and Leggit and I start sleeping in the patchwork van. It's quieter, it's got mattresses and you don't get drunken revellers stumbling over you in the middle of the night. Every night, Mouse and I crash out on separate bunks, formal and polite. Every night, when it's still and dark and quiet, Mouse burrows in under my quilt and we snuggle up. He's so small and skinny you hardly notice him. After a while, I get so I can't sleep properly unless I know he's there.

Is this what it feels like to have a brother?

Mouse doesn't scowl so much these days, and Finn drags him into the shower occasionally, so it's possible to see his tanned, freckly skin beneath the grime. He smells faintly of chocolate, which can't be bad.

If you walk up past the main festival field, cross the lane and follow the river into the hills, you come to a place where a long, white ribbon of waterfall crashes down into a deep, silver-blue pool. The water roars and foams and the pool is icy cold, even on days when the sun is hot.

An old horse chestnut tree hangs over the water, and you can climb right up into its branches and disappear into a cool, green world where the leaves brush your skin like dry fingers.

It's our special place, Finn and Mouse and Leggit and me. We come here when we want some peace, away from the festival noise and hassle. Sometimes, Cara and Kai hang out here, too, and occasionally Tess and Storm come up to swim, but mostly it's just us. When we've had enough of music and juggling and bonfires and boozed-up hippies, we come here.

Mouse can't swim. Finn and I stand for ages in the icy pool beneath the waterfall, towing him about with a hand beneath his chin, getting him to relax and float or kick his legs like a frog. His body is stiff, one spindly leg always trailing the bottom as a safety net. He's not a natural. Without the hand under the chin, he would sink like a stone, but he won't give up.

When he's had enough of the water, Mouse crawls out and sits on a rock to dry out. He practises his juggling with three velvet beanbags Tess made for him, and he's getting really good.

He throws sticks for Leggit to fetch, skims stones, builds dams. He climbs up beside the roaring waterfall, clinging to rocks that are slippy and green with slime. He makes a rope-swing in the horse chestnut tree and swoops across the pool, his feet skimming the surface.

Sometimes, when he thinks we're not looking, he gets out a box of matches and strikes them, one after the other, letting them burn right down until the flames lick his fingertips. He stares at the flame, mesmerized, then drops them into the water. Whenever I catch him, I take the matches away and give him a lecture, but Mouse just shrugs and the next day, or the day after, he'll have another box of matches and the whole spooky game starts again. He looks fearless. Anyone who hadn't heard him cry in the night would think that he was.

I'm happy here, but there's just one problem. We're six days into the Tree People Festival, and there's still no sign of Dad. When I ask Storm what's happening, she gets all evasive and grumpy.

'How do *I* know when he'll turn up?' she says. 'He said he'd be here, so he'll be here. Or maybe he'll catch us at the next place, who knows?'

'What's the next place?' I ask.

'I don't know, Dizz. There's a gathering down in Somerset, there's Womad in Reading . . . or we could head over to Yorkshire for the Green World Festival. Can't you just stop worrying about your dad?'

'But how will he know where to find us?'

'I'll let him know, Dizzy, OK? Come on, you need to stop hassling him and relax.'

'You did remember to post my cards? The one from the launderette and the one I bought from the Greenpeace stall?'

'*Yes*. I'm sure. Look, Dizz, take some advice. Don't pester your dad. Ever think he might be enjoying some time on his own?'

I frown, because that's one thought I really haven't hit on before. Could she be right? Could Dad be making the most of his time out from being a single parent?

'I just miss him,' I trail off sadly. 'I just wondered when he'd be here.'

'*I* don't know, Dizzy, what am I, a fortune-teller or what?' she huffs.

'Well . . . yes.' I nod at the faded sign on the door of the patchwork van, which says 'Tarot readings, £5'.

Storm rolls her eyes. 'I guess you still believe in Santa Claus, too. Grow up.'

She turns her back and walks away, and my eyes prick with the injustice of it all.

Later, up at the waterfall, Finn sits with his back against the horse chestnut tree, playing my guitar, soaking up the sun. He is showing me new songs, busking songs.

'When you play in the streets, you need to grab people's attention pretty quick,' he says. 'You don't want them to walk past. Sad songs are good, old songs.'

He plays 'Hey Jude', 'Wonderwall' and 'Yellow'. His voice is soft and strong, his brown fingers long and graceful as they pick out the chords. It sounds professional.

'Worth 10p?' he asks.

'Nah. I'm saving up for a Cliff Richard CD,' I tell him.

Finn pulls a mock-hurt face and hands over the guitar. I've been practising loads this holiday, and I launch into the chords for Robbie Williams' 'Angels'. I make no mistakes, but Finn is a slave-driver.

'Sing,' he says. 'Go on.'

I start off with a thin, reedy wail, then settle into it a little. I can do it as long as I focus on the guitar and refuse to look at Finn. He's bound to be laughing. I remember how Jade and I got thrown out of the primary school choir, aged eight, for talking too much. Or was it because I had a rotten voice and they didn't know how to tell me? I've never been sure.

'Not bad,' Finn says, and when I peer out from behind my veil of hair, he looks serious. He's definitely not laughing, anyway. 'Try again.'

So I sing it again, and Finn gets his tin whistle and tries out a few sounds. He works up a soft, flutey trill to go with the chorus.

'A winner,' he says. 'Didn't know you could sing. We'll clean up!'

'Clean up where?'

'In town, when we go busking. You can get a bus in if you're up early enough – the bus stop is down the lane, by the crossroads. There's one in every morning, another one back late in the afternoon. Fancy a day out?'

I look at my toes. A day in town would be great, but what if it's the day that Dad turns up? I've waited so long already I can't risk missing him.

'Problem?' Finn asks, gently.

'No. No problem,' I lie. 'It's just – I don't know if I fancy busking. I'd be too scared to sing in front of people. And who'll mind Mouse and Leggit while we're away?'

'We'll take them with us,' Finn says. 'Mouse'll love it. We can busk a bit – you don't have to sing if you don't want to – then we'll grab some lunch and hit the beach. I thought you'd like it.'

He leans forwards and tucks a corkscrew strand of hair behind my ear. His blue-grey eyes look into mine, seeing past the excuses. 'I thought you could maybe find a phone box and ring your dad,' he whispers.

I fling an arm round his neck and hug him tight. It's different from hugging a girl. Finn smells of long grass and waterfalls and warm skin. His matted hair feels surprisingly soft and heavy under my fingertips.

'It's OK,' he whispers into my neck. 'I promise, Dizz, it'll be OK.'

I'm up at seven, crouching outside Tess and Finn's tent, tugging on a length of damp string that snakes through the grass and disappears inside the tent through a tiny gap in the door-zip. I tug again. There's something heavy on the other end, and then there's a grunt and the string goes loose and I know Finn's awake. The string is his alarm clock, tied round his big toe.

By the time he crawls into the patchwork van, Mouse and I are slurping Weetabix and soya milk.

'Hi,' he says, his eyes sleepy, his dreads sticking out at right angles.

I remember how weird it was, yesterday, to touch those matted snakes of hair. Then I blush, and try to forget.

'Hi,' I say briskly. 'Breakfast's ready.'

Finn scoops up his bowl and flops on to the bunk where Leggit is lying, upside down, long legs pointed towards the van roof. She catches a whiff of the cereal and scrabbles back to an upright position. Her head rests on Finn's shoulder, brown eyes fixed on the bowl, a sliver of white fang showing. Finn reaches up to the cupboard and pours some dog biscuits on the floor for Leggit to hoover up.

It takes half an hour to walk down to the bus stop, fifteen minutes more before the tiny, ramshackle coach appears. Mouse sticks his tongue out at a staring passenger. I clutch Storm's fringey purple scarf, looped around Leggit's collar instead of a lead. She barks in excitement as the door swoops open.

'Bringing that dog on? You'll have to pay half fare for it,' the driver says gruffly.

'No problem,' says Finn, stepping forwards with the cash. The driver stares at Finn's bare feet for a long moment before ringing up the fares.

We bundle Leggit on to the bus and shove her into a seat. She writhes around and finally settles down in the aisle. Every time someone gets on or off, they have to step over her. The bus clatters around the countryside for ages, picking up a man in a business suit from the end of a farm-track, two backpackers wilting under the weight of their rucksacks and a trio of old ladies with matching nylon cardies and shopping trollies.

By the time we shudder to a halt at the bus

station in town, it's just past nine. Ayr is buzzing. Shops are opening up, cafés are dragging tables out on to the pavement. It's going to be hot, and it's going to be busy. A perfect busking day, Finn says.

Finn, Mouse and Leggit take a trawl down the main street, looking for a good place to settle. I go looking for a phone box.

'Want us to stay?' Finn asks, but I wave him away.

I stand in the phone box, stacking up my 20ps neatly. I cough, pick up the receiver, check outside to make sure there's no queue. I push a coin into the slot. It feels weird ringing home from a musty phone box in a strange town. I wish I'd asked Finn to wait.

My fingers tremble as they push the buttons, and the ring tone sounds extra loud in my ear.

The receiver clicks and clears and a woman's voice says, 'Hi! Lucy here.'

*Lucy*. Dad's girlfriend.

I hold the receiver away from my face. What's she doing there? Where's Dad? Lucy never stays overnight at the flat. So what's she doing there so early, what's she doing answering our phone like she's done it a million times before?

'Hello? Is there anyone there?' she says. 'Who *is* this?'

I put a hand over my mouth, squeeze my eyes shut and let my face fall against the cool metal of the telephone. I try to remember to breathe.

'Hello?' Lucy says again. 'Dizzy, Dizzy, is that you? Please speak to me! Don't hang up! I'll just get your dad, he's in the shower . . .'

I hear her calling 'Pete, Pete!' in the background. The receiver slips through my fingers, dangling on its long silver cord. I remember what Storm said yesterday. *Maybe your dad is enjoying the break, Dizzy. Ever think of that?*

I press down the button to cut off the call, and replace the receiver with a shaky hand.

It's just gone nine, and Lucy is at the flat while Dad's in the shower. I can't kid myself. She stayed over. She never did that while I was there, but now that I'm not . . . Maybe she'll move in. Maybe they don't miss me at all.

That's why Dad hasn't come – because he's busy playing house with his girlfriend, taking a break from me. He's having fun. He'll come and get me, sometime, sure. Definitely before the new term starts. But right now, he's in no hurry to trade his freedom for parenthood. He's happy. Without me.

There's a sharp rapping on the phone-box door.

'You all right?' a woman calls, her pink face too close to the glass.

I push out of the booth, past the woman. My

throat prickles with hurt. I feel stupid, idiotic, crazy for worrying about my dad, for stressing out over whether he had the right address for the festival, whether Storm put a first-class stamp on my postcards. For missing him.

I want him to miss me back, to rescue me from the patchwork van and the lazy, aimless, muddy world of festivals and travellers and soya milk and stale bread with little patches of green mould.

Too bad. It's not going to happen.

I find a big department store and drift in, hunting down the loos. I fill a sink with cold water and splash my face, drying it on my T-shirt. A woman with a mop and bucket, cleaning the cubicles, tries not to stare. I rake a comb through my tangled hair and hold my head high.

Outside, I follow the sound of twanging guitar strings and find Mouse, Finn and Leggit installed in an alcove outside Marks & Spencer, tuning up. They've spread a stripy rug across the pavement and Leggit is stretched out like a small, spiky-haired antelope. Mouse sits dreamily, licking a huge ice-cream cornet adorned with chocolate flakes and two colours of sticky sauce.

'OK?' Finn grins.

'Don't ask.'

Finn, who knows when to push it and when not to, doesn't.

We warm up slowly, with Finn on the tin whistle, churning out folky tunes and Irish ballads and ancient hippy songs from the land that time forgot. Mouse sets Finn's black sunhat at the front of the stripy rug to collect the cash. A shopper hurls in 10p, then a toddler drops in some coppers. Finn relaxes, gets into the music. The hat fills slowly.

I nip down the street to WHSmith and buy cans of Coke, water for Leggit and a *Beano* for Mouse. Strolling back, I notice the way Mouse is sitting, sad-eyed, shoulders hunched, pale and small and skinny. Every mum that passes him looks back, looks worried, digs into her purse.

'Have you done this before?' I ask him.

'Course,' he says. 'Loads of times, with Mum. Only without the music.'

'Oh.'

Begging.

Sometimes, Mouse makes me feel about a hundred years old.

I hand him the *Beano*, break open the Cokes, pour water into an empty ice-cream tub from the gutter for Leggit. We settle in for the morning.

The streets fill up with tourists, Mouse flicks through his comic listlessly and Finn runs through his list of surefire winners, strumming the guitar or letting me play while he sings. Cash drips steadily into the hat.

People smile as they walk past, a few kids stop and watch, a middle-aged woman gives us a two-pound coin and tells us 'Stand by Me' is her all-time favourite song. A stern-faced bloke gives us a large tin of Chappie, 'For the poor old dog'.

'She's meant to be thin,' Mouse protests. 'She's a lurcher.'

I get brave and try 'Angels' with Finn on tin whistle, and for a whole three minutes I manage to blot out the phone call and Lucy's bright, simpering voice and the fact that Dad's not coming, not any time soon. Like I care.

Then Mouse spots a couple of policemen over the road, and we grab our stuff and melt into the crowd of shoppers. We've made almost twelve quid! Mouse waits while Finn and I dive into a bakery. We buy sandwiches, crisps, pop, chocolate, custard doughnuts.

'All set, then,' says Finn, outside. 'Let's find the beach!'

Mouse whoops and his whole face lights up. He wraps Leggit's scarf-lead round his wrist and skips off along the pavement. I spot his *Beano* in the gutter, dip down to retrieve it. 'Mouse,' I call after him. 'You forgot this!'

'Don't bother,' Finn says, snatching the comic away and dropping it into a wastepaper bin. 'He won't miss it.'

'He might,' I argue, but Finn fixes me with a sad, grey-eyed glance.

'He won't,' he says firmly. 'Didn't you notice? The kid can't read.'

Finn asks directions to the beach, and we cut down a series of side streets until we see the seawall and a vast, rolling slash of deep-blue ocean. Mouse is silent, his eyes huge, nostrils flared. He looks like he could explode with excitement.

'Look,' he whispers to Leggit. 'That's the beach! That's the *sea*!'

'Have you never seen the sea before?' Finn asks.

'Of course. *Loads*,' Mouse says, scornfully. 'Don't think Leggit has, though.'

Finn and I exchange grins.

We trip down the steps to the beach, stumble through the soft, silvery sand. Leggit squirms, slithering free of the fringey scarf. She sprints off down the beach, zigzagging wildly through the football games, sunbathers, kids with buckets and spades. Down at the water's edge, she finds a huge piece of seaweed and shakes it about violently, then charges up to Mouse and drops it at his feet.

'*Sea*weed,' he says, amazed.

Finn, barefoot and wearing skate shorts, is already paddling through the shallows, chucking driftwood sticks for Leggit to chase.

Mouse and I pull off our trainers and socks, roll up our jeans. The soft sand is hot, it squidges through your toes, tickles your feet. Mouse runs down to the water's edge, shuts his eyes and lets the tide wash over his feet. I've never seen him look so happy.

We turn to the right, trailing along the edge of the sea until we find a quiet bit of beach, away from the picnics, the swimmers, the deckchairs. We spread the stripy rug, tip the picnic out of its bag, bask in the sun.

'Is this why they're called *sand*wiches?' Finn asks, after Mouse skids to a halt beside him, spraying his egg mayonnaise.

'Sorry,' says Mouse, then laughs when he sees that Finn isn't cross. When he smiles, he's almost cute.

We eat till we're stuffed. Leggit has a roast chicken triple-layer with salad, plus one of the custard doughnuts. Then she skitters back to the water's edge, where Mouse is building a sand-castle studded with mismatched shells and circled with stumps of driftwood.

'He's happy,' I say.

'Yeah.'

Mouse draws zigzags in the wet sand with a stick, digs a moat round the castle with his bare hands, drapes seaweed from his ears and roars at us like a sea monster. He runs in circles with Leggit, wades fully clothed into the sea up to his waist and staggers out, dripping. His wet, brown limbs are crusted with gold, his damp hair dusty with sand.

Mouse looks like any other kid on the beach – maybe a bit skinnier, a bit scruffier, a bit more nervous. But he's having fun, and I know and Finn knows that it's an awful long time since Mouse had fun.

'So, what did your dad say?' Finn asks at last.

I drop down into the sand, close my eyes. In the distance, a baby is crying, and the sound of an ice-cream van drifts down from the street.

'Change of plan,' I say lightly to the pale-blue sky. 'He's not coming, now. Not till the end of the summer.'

'What happened?'

'Oh, y'know. He's taking some time out to be with his girlfriend, Lucy. She's really nice. He says that I might as well make the most of my time with Storm. Enjoy the summer, that kind of thing.'

Well, that's what he'd have said if I'd given him the chance. If I tell Finn I hung up without even talking to Dad, he'll march me down to the phone box and make me ring back, just to be sure I haven't jumped to the wrong conclusions. I can't do that. I've spent eight years knowing my mum abandoned me when I was four. I won't get through another day if I think Dad's ditched me, too. He's entitled to spend some time out with Lucy. It doesn't mean he doesn't love me any more.

'You OK with that?' Finn watches me from under the brim of his black cotton hat.

'Sure, why not? Lucy's cool. And I'm having fun. Getting to know Storm. It's *good* for me and Dad to have some time apart.'

'Is it?'

If Finn doesn't stop looking at me, I'm going to cry.

'Yes,' I say defiantly. 'Yes, it is.'

I roll over on to my front and stare down at the sand. Crying is a bad plan. It'd only make the sand wet.

'Custard doughnut?' Finn suggests, offering me the box. 'Seriously wicked. Go on – Leggit recommends them.'

I laugh, lifting out the last custard doughnut. It's soft and sweet and soggy, and slightly gritty with sand. It tastes great.

We have to drag Mouse away from the beach.

'Come *on*,' Finn threatens. 'We'll miss the last bus. We've been here all afternoon.'

'Just a bit longer?' Mouse whines.

'No way. We told Tess we'd get shopping – y'know, bread and fruit and chocolate spread. If we don't go now, we won't have time!'

'*Please?*'

Neither of us have ever heard Mouse say please before. For anything. Finn sighs, defeated.

'Half an hour,' I tell Mouse. 'Then we really, really have to go. Promise?'

'Promise.'

We make the bus station with seven minutes to spare. The bus is in, half-full, the driver reading a newspaper.

'Time for a quick ice cream?' Finn says, and we tie Leggit to a lamp post and duck into the nearest sweetshop. Finn picks out two Magnums and orders a cornet with flakes and strawberry sauce for Mouse. He pays. The man at the counter frowns.

'Nice day,' I say, trying out a Finn tactic.

'Hmmph,' says the man, moving over to guard the open door.

Mouse has drifted down to the back of the shop. He trails Finn's rucksack, half-full of seaweed, pebbles and shells, behind him. His fingers stray over the packets of blow-up lilos, beach balls, buckets and spades. He strokes a pair of red rubber flippers and a snorkel.

'Come on, Mouse,' I hiss. 'Gotta go. Can't miss that bus.'

I step out into the sunshine, Finn on my heels. Then Mouse bursts past us like a small explosion, the rucksack on his back.

'Quick,' he shouts, halfway up the street. 'Run! Run! Leggit, c'mon!'

'Oi! Stop!' shouts the shop man. Finn charges past me, and in the confusion, Leggit drags herself free of the lamp post and hurtles off after them. My heart thumps and my mouth feels like saw-dust. I want to run, I try to run, but my legs are like jelly.

Two Magnums and a huge cornet lie melting on the pavement.

'Finn!' I shriek, but then the shop man grabs me by the hem of my T-shirt. If I was brave enough, I'd bash him with my guitar.

'Back inside, young *lady*,' he says sneerily.

'Finn!'

I look over my shoulder and see Finn bowl up level with Mouse, grab him round the waist and whirl him round. Leggit is leaping about wildly, crashing into shoppers and tourists, and yelping hopelessly. Behind them, I see the bus shudder to life and crawl slowly out of the bus station.

The shop man marches me back inside. A couple of shoppers stare.

'OK, Jan, ring the police,' the man says gruffly. 'I'm sick of this. The police, OK?'

The shop darkens briefly as Finn appears in the doorway, with Mouse in front of him.

Outside, Leggit is scoffing down the last of the ice cream.

19

Everyone stares as we troop through the shop into a dingy backroom office. I wish I could hold my head high, like Finn. No, actually, I wish the floor would open and swallow me up. My face is so pink you could toast marshmallows in the heat from my cheeks.

Leggit skids into the room just as the door slams shut, her face sticky with ice cream. The shopkeeper snorts in disgust. 'Sorry now, aren't you?' he says to us, nastily. 'Well, too bad, it's too late for that. Put that bag down – I'd like the police to see what you've got in there.'

We stare at the rucksack Mouse is carrying, the bag he stuffed with bits of driftwood and stuff from the beach. The bag he's hanging on to for dear life. It's fuller, heavier than it should be. It doesn't take a genius to figure out why.

'Oh, Mouse.'

He drops the rucksack and flings his arms round

me. I hold him tight. Finn looks at me over Mouse's head, eyes wide.

The shopkeeper tips the contents of the rucksack out across the floor. Along with the grey toy mouse, the driftwood, feathers, seaweed, there are learn-to-swim armbands, a blow-up beach ball, a water pistol, goggles, a yellow plastic spade, six boxes of matches, four Mars bars and a disposable camera.

'Forget to pay for a few things, did you?'

'It was a mistake,' Finn says. 'We can sort it out.'

'Yeah, when the police get here,' the shopkeeper says. 'I've seen it all before. Buy something small, try to distract me while you let the little kid do your dirty work. Bloody cheek. It's *stealing*, you know!'

'I know,' says Finn sadly.

'Empty your pockets,' says the shopkeeper.

The police arrive while we're turfing out bus tickets, chewing gum, fluff, shells, loose change. It's the same two we saw when we were busking. One of them rolls his eyes, and I know they've recognized us, too.

There's a long conversation about whether the shopkeeper is going to press charges. 'They may only be kids, but they're still criminals,' he says.

'Right. Well, certainly, shoplifting is a very serious affair,' the red-haired policeman says. 'We'll be taking these characters down to the station, and of course we'll be calling their parents in.'

'But?'

'But the boy who actually stole the goods – well, he's just a kid,' the policeman says. 'Have they taken stuff from you before?'

The shopkeeper stares at us for a long, long time. 'No,' he admits at last. 'I've never seen them before. You can tell from their accents they're not local. I mean, just *look* at them. Dirty, stinking hippies.'

'That's quite enough, sir,' the podgy policeman says. 'Come on, you lot. Let's get you down to the station and get hold of your mums and dads.'

We get to ride to the station in a police car. Leggit leaves sand and smears of strawberry sauce all over the back seats. The policemen lecture us about stealing, along with threats that next time we risk a court case, a fine, a police record.

'I know,' Finn says. 'We're very sorry. Mouse didn't know what he was doing. It's not his fault. I think he thought I'd already paid, and I didn't realize . . .'

'Sure,' says the red-haired policeman. 'Just don't let there be a next time.'

'There won't be,' I say. 'Will there?'

'No,' Mouse whispers.

Once we're at the police station, things get complicated. We tell them our names, and they think it's a wind-up.

'Finn, Dizzy, Mouse?' the policeman says. 'Mouse, as in Mickey? C'mon, son, you can do better than that.'

'It's his name,' Finn shrugs. 'Really.'

'OK. Mouse. Mouse what?'

But nobody knows Mouse's surname, not even Mouse himself. At least if he does, he's not saying. It gets worse. Our address makes no sense to the policemen. We live in a van, a tent, a tepee, somewhere in the South Ayrshire hills.

'It's the Tree People Festival,' Finn explains.

'Right,' says the podgy policeman. 'Great. And is there a mobile number where we can contact your parents? No? Thought not. Oh, well.'

So we drive back to the festival in the back of a police car. No sirens, no handcuffs, no blue flashing lights, just us and two policemen who are probably hacked off they have to drive out into the middle of nowhere when they planned simply to ring our parents and get us picked up from the police station. We've probably ruined their evening. Then again, they haven't exactly done great things for ours.

We drive in beneath the Tree People banner and across the rutted field. Travellers blink sleepily at the car, or stare, hostile, curious. One bloke drops a spliff into the grass and grinds it underfoot. A man dressed up with stilts and face-paint blows giant soap bubbles at the windscreen.

The police car gets stuck in a maze of tents, and we get out.

'We'll be OK from here,' Finn says. 'Thanks very much.'

'What am I, a taxi service?' the red-haired policeman laughs. 'Nice try, kid. We need to see your parents. Now.'

We weave through the tents and stalls, taking the scenic route to the tepee. No sign of Tess, Storm or Zak.

'OK,' says Finn. 'This is it.'

He nods towards the tepee, points towards the doorflap.

'This?' asks the podgy policeman.

'Yep.'

They step inside, we follow.

The tepee reeks of joss sticks and some kind of incense that's been sprinkled on the fire. Tess, Storm, Zak and an assorted bunch of crusties are sitting around, drumming out a low, hollow beat and singing a wailing, hippy chant. Just an average evening at the festival, then.

Storm leaps to her feet, terrified. Zak stubs out his spliff and follows.

'What's wrong, man?' he says. 'Mouse? You been in trouble again?'

Tess stands up and starts ushering the drummers out of the tepee. 'Everything's fine, we just need some space,' she tells them. 'We'll get this sorted. Gentlemen,' she turns to the policemen. 'Can I offer you something to drink? Tea? Coffee? Elder-flower cordial?'

The policemen sip coffee with soya milk and tell Tess, Zak and Storm that they need to keep a closer eye on us, make sure we understand the difference between right and wrong.

'We *do*,' Finn says. 'Honestly, officer. It was all a mistake.'

'The little kid isn't so clear, though, is he?'

'He had a rough start in life,' Zak says. 'A lot to cope with, y'know? But he's getting better. He's getting some real values here.'

The policemen exchange quick glances, but they don't say anything. Storm looks nervous and pushes her dope tin out of sight, under a cushion.

'Discipline is what he needs,' the red-haired policeman is saying. 'Clear boundaries, routine. Supervision.'

'Yes, of course, officer,' Tess says. 'It won't happen again.'

'If it does, then it's just a matter of time before the social services get involved,' the policeman warns. 'If they consider he's not being looked after properly, they could even take him into care. I'm not saying it'll happen, but it's something you should be aware of.'

'It won't come to that,' Tess says firmly.

'No *way*, man,' Zak echoes.

'Let's hope not.'

The policemen go, picking their way through the tents and campfires, stared at by small scruffy kids and glowering crusties. Someone has painted a rainbow on the bonnet of their car. The podgy policeman shakes his head and wipes it off with a large white hanky.

'Take care,' calls the red-haired one, as they drive out across the rutted field. 'Stay out of trouble.'

'We will!' I shout, and we run after the car, waving. Even Mouse.

Staying out of trouble is tough, though, because right now we're up to our ears in it. Bringing police on to the festival site is bad news. How many spliffs and tins of dope are there on site? How many vans or trucks without road tax or insurance, with dodgy tyres or an out-of-date MOT?

It's lucky they weren't interested in anything apart from us, that they didn't get mad about the rainbow on the car. They were OK. All the same, there'll be a row, a showdown, a slanging match. It was Mouse who messed up, but Finn and I were in charge and we blew it. We forgot for a while that Mouse is trouble. We thought we could trust him when we should have known better.

Back at the tepee, Storm is stressing out. 'We have to go,' she's saying to anyone who'll listen. 'They'll be back, they'll bust us for drugs and find something wrong with the van and they'll take

Mouse away . . . you heard what they said. We have to move on, now.'

Tess hovers at the edge of the tepee, watching the drama, trying to stay out of it. Quietly, she puts an arm round Mouse.

'Not *now*,' Zak says. 'Not yet. We'll take a day or two, pack up slowly, decide what to do next. They won't be back. Chill out.'

'Now,' says Storm. 'We have to go now. Did you give them Pete's address?' she asks me, her face pale. She looks older, somehow. Anxious.

'No, we just said we were staying here, at the festival.'

'That's something, then. Pete would go mad if he knew. He'd say I wasn't looking after you properly. He'd say I was letting you run wild . . .'

Maybe he would. Maybe I am. But Dad doesn't know, because he's busy having fun with Lucy, watching slushy films on Sky Box Office and eating takeaway pizza, or whatever you do on grown-up dates. If he was bothered, he'd be here by now, wouldn't he?

'Who cares what Dad thinks?' I tell Storm, stroking the soft, velvet fuzz at the back of her head. 'It wasn't like that, was it? We're OK. Aren't we?'

Storm smiles, but her eyes are distant. She pulls away from me and starts running around the tepee, rolling up quilts, piling up cushions, folding rugs.

'Look, Storm, we're not going now, OK?' Zak argues. 'We'll move on if it makes you happy, first thing tomorrow. But not now. It's getting dark. This doesn't make sense, Storm. There's no need.'

'There's every need. I've got a feeling. Really. A bad feeling. It's time to go, Zak. *Please.*'

Zak takes a deep breath in. He rakes a brown, skinny hand through his long, fair hair and his green eyes swoop over Finn and Mouse and me. He looks seriously hacked off.

'OK,' he says at last. 'OK. But we can't take the tepee down in the middle of the night, can we?'

'Leave it,' Storm says. 'Let Amber take care of it for a bit. Carl's got a truck, they can stash the larch poles in that. They're going down to the Blue River Camp in Somerset, we can meet them there.'

'But that's not till August . . .'

Storm stops packing and looks directly at Tess. 'We could stay at your place,' Storm says. 'We could stay at the cottage, just for a week or so, on the way down. Couldn't we? Tess?'

Tess ruffles Mouse's hair. Like me, like Zak, I know she'll agree to anything to put the smile back on Storm's face. 'Course you can,' she says. 'You know that. No problem. We'll all go, shall we? Finn?'

'Yeah,' Finn agrees. 'We'll all go.'

His fingers squeeze mine in the shadows of the tepee.

'OK,' Zak says finally, defeated. 'OK.'

It's chaos then. We pack the van, stuffing in bags and boxes and rucksacks and quilts. We take down Tess's tent and pack up the car. Then we sit around drinking herb tea with Amber and Carl to talk about leaving the tepee with them and meeting up down south. Dozens of people file in to hug us and wish us well. Cara gives me a daisy-chain necklace.

It's midnight before we set off, Tess's car first, the patchwork van rattling along behind. We lurch slowly through the field, passing out beneath the faded Tree People banner and into the lane. The red tail lights of Tess's car disappear in the distance and we're alone, me and Mouse and Leggit squashed into the back of the patchwork van, Zak and Storm up front.

It seems like a million years since we sat in the sun on the beach at Ayr, since we paddled in the salt water and ate custard doughnuts flecked with sand. Mouse snuggles up against my shoulder. I lean back, trying to stay awake by watching the road, sliding into sleep all the same.

When I wake, we're parked in a pool of light on the edge of a service-station car park. We stumble out of the van, use the loos, then trail into the all-night restaurant. We spot Tess and Finn in the far corner, scoffing chips and beans. We wave. Zak orders two black coffees. It's four in the morning and the smell of fast food makes my stomach growl.

'I'm starving,' says Mouse. 'Can we have chips? A Coke, even?'

'Seen the price of it?' snaps Zak. 'No chance.'

We slump into a booth alongside Tess and Finn. Storm looks around the café, checking out the other diners. A lorry driver eating egg and chips, a sleepy family huddled over huge baguettes, a lone woman sipping coffee and staring at a chocolate muffin.

Finn slides out of his seat just as the lorry driver leaves the café. He scoops up the leftover chips and a plate of untouched bread and butter, bringing them back to us. 'Early breakfast?' he says.

'Isn't that stealing?' Mouse asks, amazed.

'No,' says Tess. 'Not really, because the man already paid for that food. He just didn't eat it all. I think it's more like . . . recycling.'

I open my eyes wide, and Finn winks at me.

The coffee-and-cake woman gets up to leave.

'Chocolate muffin, anyone?' Tess whispers, and Mouse is off like a shot to rescue the abandoned cake before anyone can clear it away.

We sit in the café for over an hour, recycling chips, baguettes, scones and fresh fruit salad, before a tired-looking assistant in a red waistcoat notices and asks us to leave. Mouse, a natural at this game, snaffles a serviette full of abandoned sausages for Leggit on the way out.

We drive off into the drizzly pink dawn, singing.

I imagined a chocolate-box cottage with roses round the door, but Bramble Cottage is pure hippy heaven. There are roses round the door, sure, but also nettles taller than I am, and a cool-eyed billy goat (Cedric) chewing mouthfuls of sweet peas. There are chickens in the vegetable patch, eggs under the hedge and frogs croaking in the pond. A large tabby cat is asleep on top of the compost heap.

A grey-haired woman in a dressing gown and slippers comes out along the garden path, snipping flowers and eating toast and jam.

'Mum!' Tess shouts, and flings her arms round the woman. I watch Finn hug his gran and I'm stabbed with jealousy, homesickness, loneliness. I want Dad. Right now, I'd even tolerate Lucy. Maybe.

Instead, I have to make do with Storm and Zak, and I wonder why it's not enough. I thread a hand through Mouse's. He's looking as lost as I feel.

It's hard to resist the atmosphere at Tess's place, all the same. Storm and Zak must be regular visitors here, because they park the van in the 'usual place' under the apple trees and start making it homey right away, hanging wind chimes from the lowest branches and spreading rugs and quilts out across the grass.

'This is better,' Storm says, flinging herself down on to the grass, gazing up at the soft blue sky. 'We're *safe* here. We can just hang out for a while, chill, rest, get sorted for Somerset.'

'No money to be made,' Zak says, sulkily.

'Stop stressing,' says Storm. 'We can sign on. We don't need much.'

'Just as well.'

Finn's brother, Niall, a six-foot version of Finn with a black Mohican, black nail varnish and a pierced tongue, makes a huge veggie fry-up and we squash in round the scrubbed pine table in Tess's kitchen and eat until we're stuffed. Finn's gran wafts about the place in crinkly skirts with bells on, a purple bandana wrapped around her long, grey hair. I'm beginning to forget what normal people look like.

I'm beginning to forget a lot of things.

Hi Dad,

Thought I'd better let you know we've moved again. We're at Tess's place now, Bramble Cottage, for the next few weeks. I'll get Storm to put the proper address on the bottom of this card, in case you want to get in touch or anything. It'd be great to see you, if you're not too busy. And Lucy, of course. I'm still missing you – hope you haven't forgotten me.

    Love,

        Dizzy xxxx

There's a tree house in a rickety old oak behind the cottage. It's a simple tree house, no roof, nothing fancy, just a wide platform of smooth pine planks with a rail running round the edge and a frayed rope-ladder dangling.

Mouse loves it. 'I'm sleeping here,' he says.

'No way,' I tell him. 'It's too high, too rickety, and there's no roof . . .'

'*I* used to,' shrugs Finn.

A couple of nights later we're holed up there, the three of us, wrapped in quilts and sleeping bags, sipping hot apple juice from chipped tin mugs. Jam-jar lanterns swing from the branches, dropping thin pools of light around us.

Leggit whines and howls so much that Finn has to haul her up the swinging rope-ladder, too, a skinny bundle of wriggling bones and sticky-up hair. She sits with her head over the rail, listening to the goat rooting about in the bushes below.

'I like it here,' Mouse says into the darkness.

'Me, too,' I tell him.

'Me, three,' Finn says.

'We can see *everything*,' Mouse says.

I lean back and gaze up through the leaves, looking at the stars. It's funny how the skies are bigger, darker, when you're in the country. The night is velvet-blue, not neon-orange. I pick out the shape of the Big Dipper and find the Pole Star. I show Finn and Mouse, and explain how it's always there, no matter what. A magical star, like Storm says.

'Magical,' Mouse echoes. Then, 'Nobody can get us here.'

'Who'd want to?' Finn asks, surprised. 'There's nothing to be scared of.'

But maybe, for Mouse, there is.

'Bad people,' he says in a small voice.

'There *are* no bad people here,' I tell him.

'You wouldn't let them get me, anyway,' he whispers.

'No way,' says Finn. 'I'll fight 'em off with a big stick, set Leggit on them, pour boiling oil on their heads. Hot apple juice, anyway. I'll look after you, Mouse, little mate.'

'Me, too,' I echo. 'Always.'

'Always,' Mouse breathes.

His eyes flutter shut and he burrows down beneath the quilt. The grey toy mouse surfaces, clutched in one tiny, grubby hand. I wonder what he dreams about. I wonder who the bad people are.

'Grandad made this tree house,' Finn is saying. 'When we first came back here, when I was seven. For me and Niall. We thought it was the best thing we'd ever seen in our lives.'

'He's not around any more?'

'He died a couple of years back.'

'I'm sorry.'

'It's OK,' Finn says. 'I miss him like mad, but I'll never forget him. He taught me to play the piano, to love music. I had the chance to know him, to know which bits of me I got from him.'

I stare up through the leaves, counting stars. Finn has picked up his guitar, a tattier version of mine, and starts picking out chords.

'D'you ever think about your dad?' I ask.

Finn shrugs. 'He left before I was born. Why should I care about him? He couldn't even hang around long enough to see his own son.'

'D'you think it's a traveller thing?' I ask. 'You know, all this stuff about freedom and fun and moving on?'

Finn frowns in the darkness. 'Maybe, some-times,' he says. 'Mostly, though, I think it's just a *people* thing.'

Finn's picking out the tune to an old Linkin Park song, 'Somewhere I Belong'. I've never heard it before, but when Finn plays it, it's the best, the saddest song in the world.

Does *anyone* know where they belong? I used to think I did. I belonged with Dad, in our flat in Birmingham. I belonged with my mates, messing about at school, drinking Cokes in Dimitri's caff, sunbathing in the back garden, talking on the phone till all hours. Then Storm turned up and took me away, and now I don't belong anywhere.

'I used to dream Storm would come back,' I say. 'Then she did. It's what I always wanted, only now I'm not so sure. Is that ungrateful?'

'Nah,' Finn laughs. 'Your life just turned upside-down. You're bound to feel mixed up.'

'I thought I'd see her more, get to know her more. I thought we'd make up for lost time. I thought she'd want to know about . . . well, *me*. And she doesn't. She really doesn't. Sometimes I think I'm only here to babysit Mouse.'

'You're *not*,' Finn says. 'But . . . babysitting Mouse isn't so bad, is it?'

We look over at Mouse, the scrap of brown hair sticking out from the rolled-up quilt, the outstretched arm flung over Leggit's skinny neck.

'No, it's not bad. It's not bad at all.'

Finn puts down the guitar and leans an arm along the tree-house rail. '*Some* people care,' he says. I can feel him looking at me in the darkness, and I have to turn away.

'I think your dad cares, too,' Finn says eventually. 'What happened the other day when you rang? What did he say to upset you? You've spent weeks looking out for him, writing postcards, talking about him. Then one phone call and it's over. You'd think he's dropped off the face of the earth.'

I'm cold suddenly. I hug my knees, pulling the quilt closer round me.

'His girlfriend answered. It was only nine o'clock and his *girlfriend* answered. She never used to stay, when I was there. It felt like I'd been forgotten.'

'Dizzy!' Finn says, pulling one of the skinny plaits that hangs down by my face. 'Who could ever forget *you*? What did you say – what did *he* say?'

'Nothing. I didn't say anything. I hung up.'

Finn sighs. 'There's a phone here,' he says. 'You can ring him now. Tomorrow. Whenever.'

'Whenever,' I agree. 'Not just yet. Maybe we both need a break from each other? Him to be with Lucy, me to be here. Hey, will you play that Linkin Park thing again?'

Finn picks up the guitar and shifts position. I watch him lean in, long fingers teasing out the tune. His voice is a whisper, hardly daring to sing the words out loud. I join in with the bits I know. When he finishes, I know where I belong, and it's here and now, with Finn and Mouse and Leggit. The rest doesn't matter.

Finn hangs the guitar from a branch and stretches out his legs. His bare feet are pale in the darkness, dappled with shadows as the leaves above us shiver. One foot reaches out and prods my leg, and I catch it, hanging on to the lean, skinny shape of it. My fingers notice the rough, calloused skin on his heel and sole, the smooth skin above. I count his toenails, five little slivers of ice in the moonlight. I notice he's stopped struggling, but still, I'm slow to let go.

'Did anyone ever tell you that you have drop-dead gorgeous feet?' I ask.

Finn laughs out loud.

'No,' he says. 'Nobody ever did. Only you, Dizzy. Only you.'

It's happening again.

Eight years ago, Storm left me and went to Kathmandu with a man called Mitch. It's not Mitch, now, it's Zak, and it's not Kathmandu, it's Goa, some hippy place in India.

'Wow,' Storm says, her eyes wide. 'Wow. We're going to India, Dizz! How cool is that?'

A letter has turned up at Bramble Cottage, redirected from Zak's parents' place in Kent. It's from Zak's brother, Josh. From India. Josh has just bought a big beach house near Goa, in India. He wants Zak and Storm to come out and help him turn it into a spiritual healing centre, where hippy tourists can come to learn yoga, meditation and how to balance small chunks of crystal along their backbones. Zak, naturally, will help with this bit.

'I could do aromatherapy massage,' Storm says.

'You could if you learned it first,' Tess points out.

'How hard can it be? It's just a few oils and a bit of a back rub, isn't it? And I'm sure I could teach yoga and t'ai chi. On the beach!'

'He's talked about it before, but I never thought he'd do it,' Zak is saying. 'What a chance! And he needs me to make it work. Me and you, Storm.'

'All of us,' Storm says dreamily, flinging an arm round Mouse and me. 'What a life for the kids, growing up in the sun, walking barefoot in the sand, learning Urdu or Hindi or whatever they speak over there . . .'

'Right,' says Zak, frowning. 'The kids, too?'

'Of course, the kids too,' Storm laughs. 'We're a family, now, aren't we? We have to stick together.'

'Sure,' says Zak. 'Sure.'

Mouse takes a long drink of cold milk and wipes his mouth.

'No,' he says.

'No?' Storm falters. 'What d'you mean, no?'

Mouse shrugs, drains the milk carton and slips quickly out of the kitchen. I run after him.

We sit on the tree-house platform, swinging our legs. Finn, keeping a respectful distance, is riding his BMX in and out of the bramble bushes below, with Leggit galloping behind.

'I won't go,' Mouse says fiercely. 'They can't make me.'

'No, they can't,' I agree, but I'm not sure. Maybe they can? 'I'm not going, either. Not to *India*. I don't want to leave Dad.'

'I don't want to leave Mum,' Mouse says.

'D'you miss her much?' I ask.

Mouse shrugs. 'A bit. Sometimes.'

We look down through the leaves as Finn does a wheelie.

'She went away,' Mouse says sadly.

'She couldn't help it,' I tell him. 'She was ill. She'll get better, then she'll be able to look after you again.'

'Think so?'

'Know so.'

'Why did your dad dump you?' Mouse wants to know.

'He *didn't*. Your mum didn't, either. It's just – the way things happen. I'm spending some time with my mum, you're spending some time with your dad. Just for a while.'

Mouse frowns. 'And then I'll go back?' he asks.

'Yes.'

'But not yet?'

'No, not yet. And we're not going to India. No way.'

Beneath the tree house, Finn skids off the BMX and lands barefoot in the brambles. 'Ouch!' he yells. 'Leggit, that was your fault!'

'When I do go back to Mum's, I'll miss you,' Mouse says quietly.

'I'll miss you, too,' I tell him.

'Dizzy?'

'Mmm?'

'Are you – are you my sister? Kind of?'

I put an arm round him and he doesn't flinch away. 'I think so, Mouse,' I say. 'Kind of.'

Of course, we're not going to India.

It's not because of Mouse's mum, or my dad, but because the tickets cost £500 and children have to pay full fare. Zak says that's crazy, and Storm says, never mind, Mouse and I can come out later, once they're settled in.

'We'll just go and suss things out,' she says. 'Then, when we start earning, we'll send for you. OK, Dizz?'

But I know it's not going to happen. I'm not going to live in India, thousands of miles away from Dad, from my mates. I'm going home. Only not just yet. I'll wait till Mouse's mum is able to look after him again. *Then* I'll go.

'The kids are very welcome to stay with me for a bit,' Tess says.

'Of course,' Finn's gran chips in.

'Just for a short while,' Storm promises.

'No hassles,' says Tess.

They book the flight over the phone. Zak produces a credit card to pay for the tickets.

'Where'd he get *that*?' I whisper to Finn.

'He's loaded, Dizz, didn't you know?' Finn tells me. 'He's from a well-posh family, went to private school and everything. He and Josh, the brother, inherited a whole packet last year from some rich uncle.'

I whistle through my teeth. 'I thought they were just crusties,' I say.

'They are. Only I think they're kind of *upper* crusties.'

I think of the mouldy bread Zak made us eat, the way we had to recycle food in the service-station café. I remember him moaning about having two extra mouths to feed, even though it's always Tess who gets the shopping, makes the food, gets the clothes washed.

'Unreal,' I say.

'Tell me about it,' says Finn.

Dear Dad,
Just wanted to let you know that Storm is going to India. She might not be back for a while, so I wondered if maybe I should come home now? I'm staying with Tess and Finn and Mouse, so I'm OK,

you don't have to worry. I wish you'd write, Dad, or ring or just come and get me. I miss you so much.

Dizzy xxxxx

The day before they fly, Storm hennas her hair. She mixes a paste from hot water and foul-smelling green powder, then plasters her skinhead crop and wraps her head in cling film and towels.

'Now you,' she says.

'Me?'

'C'mon, Dizz!' she teases. 'Live dangerously!'

So she combs through my long brown curls, softly, slowly, carefully. She doesn't tug, she doesn't pull. She eases every knot and tangle loose, then smears the warm green paste over each section of hair. I close my eyes. This is what it's like, to have a mother. Someone to comb the tangles from your hair, your life.

Later, we sunbathe in the strawberry patch, eating fat, ripe berries and wiping the henna drips from our ears and necks. Niall has built a barbecue from old bricks and bits of chicken wire, and he's cooking tofu and sweetcorn and veggie kebabs in a haze of smoke. Tess is weeding in the veggie garden, Zak is reading a crystal-healing book and Mouse is trying wheelies on the BMX. Inside the cottage, Finn is playing the piano. The sound drifts out of an open window like the sound-track from a dream.

It takes an hour to wash the henna paste off my hair, another hour to dry it in the sun. Storm's hair is a fuzz of crimson velvet, mine a deep, russet shade like falling leaves, and shinier than I've ever seen it.

'Beautiful,' she says, looking at me. She roots around in Tess's sewing bag to find embroidery threads in moss green, scarlet and gold, to braid into a hair wrap. Her fingers weave through my hair quickly, gently.

'I'll remember you like this,' she says, and I know that she's saying goodbye.

Storm and Zak are gone, to a pink-walled villa on a scorching hot beach on the other side of the world. They promised to phone, to write, to send for us soon. That was three weeks back, and we're still waiting.

The patchwork van sits abandoned on the drive, a 'For sale' sign in the window. Zak tried to get Tess to buy it, the night before the flight to Goa, but she said she'd stick with the car.

'See if you can find someone who wants it,' Zak said. 'Ask for £500. And when you see Amber and Carl, ask if they'll buy the tepee. Should be worth £700, but try for more. You can send me a cheque. It'll pay for the air fares.'

Tess is sorting stuff out, tying up loose ends for Storm and Zak. It's just that there are a couple of loose ends that can't be neatly tidied away.

We stay at the cottage, Tess and Finn and Mouse and me. Tess says it's easier, less hassle than going on with the festivals. Nobody minds. Leggit chases chickens and barks at the goat and digs up the lettuces Finn's gran has planted. We're happy.

'Have you spoken to Pete lately?' Tess asks one evening. 'Did he say when he wants you back?'

'Oh, any time before school starts,' I say carelessly. 'He's not really worried. I'll ring him in a week or so.'

'Do that,' Tess says. 'Tell him to come up and stay for a few days, catch up on old times. I'm sorry he didn't make it up for the Tree People Festival.'

Finn is watching me carefully to see what I'll say. I say nothing.

'He does know where you are, doesn't he?' Tess pushes.

'Sure. I've sent him postcards, loads of them. Storm said she'd stick a letter in with the last one.'

'She did post it?' Tess frowns.

'I *think* so.'

'I hope so,' Tess says. 'I *really* hope so. Maybe I'll drop him a line myself, OK?'

'OK.'

'Ring him,' Finn says to me, later, when we're outside watering the veggie plot.

'I can't.'

'Why not? He might be worried. Does he know that Storm's done a bunk?'

'I said so on my last postcard,' I shrug.

'Ring him,' Finn says again.

'I'm scared.'

'What of?'

How do you explain it? I'm scared that Dad has forgotten me, that he's busy having fun, making the most of his freedom. I've sent him five post-cards. He knows how much I've missed him, but still he hasn't come to get me. Which has to mean that *he* hasn't missed *me*.

He knows that Storm's gone away, so why hasn't he come to rescue me? Not that I *want* to be rescued.

'*Dizzy*,' Finn says, exasperated.

I don't want to go home because it would mean leaving Mouse, and he needs me. And it would mean leaving Finn, and *I* need him. If there's such a thing as a family, we're it. Home-made, second-hand, tacked together from leftovers, but family all the same.

I stick my tongue out at Finn and he sprays me with the hosepipe, and Mouse thunders down through the cabbages on Finn's BMX to come and join in the fight. It doesn't end till we're all soaking wet, and, sadly, the cabbages are done for.

It's Finn's birthday soon.

I haven't any money to buy a present, but Tess

lets me root through her bag of scrap fabrics and I cut up a length of old blue blanket to make him a new guitar strap. In the mornings, while Finn is practising his piano or playing the guitar up in the tree house, I work on it. I fold the thick blue wool into a long, skinny rectangle. I snip a tiny hole at one end and sew a bright red shoelace to the other. Tess digs out her embroidery threads and shows me how to make stars and spirals out of satin stitch and chain stitch and little French knots.

We've built a bonfire on the lawn, and Mouse asks me if he can juggle firesticks in the evening, especially for Finn. 'Juggle, sure,' I tell him. 'Finn will love that, and you're getting really good. But not firesticks, Mouse. It's too dangerous.'

'Zak did it,' Mouse protests. 'He had those batons that were on fire, and he juggled with them. I want to do that for Finn.'

'No *way*, Mouse. Zak is much older than you. He's been juggling for years and years, and he knows that you have to treat fire with respect. It's a grown-up thing, Mouse, honestly.'

'*I* treat fire with respect,' Mouse argues.

I remember the way he is around bonfires, the way he strikes matches and lets the flames lick around his fingertips. Respect isn't the word that springs to mind.

'I *like* fire,' says Mouse.

Exactly.

'No firesticks,' I say firmly.

Mouse twists his face into a scowl, jumps on Finn's BMX and ploughs off through the flower beds.

Niall is planning a barbie for the evening, and Tess is going to make sponge cake and home-made ice cream and lemonade with real lemons.

'D'you want anyone over, on Friday?' she asks Finn. 'Kids from school?'

'No, thanks,' he answers. 'Jon's in France all summer and Danny's staying with his dad in Chester. I'm not bothered about the others.'

'OK,' Tess says easily. 'Anything special you want to do in the day? We could drive down to Lancaster to the pictures, whatever. Your call!'

'I'll think about it, OK?' Finn says.

That night, in the tree house, he asks if I'd like to take a picnic to the beach on Friday. Just us. My eyes widen. Is that 'just us', as in me and Finn? Or 'just us', as in me, Finn, Mouse and Leggit?

'The beach? I didn't know we were that near the sea. You kept that quiet!'

'It's a bus ride,' Finn shrugs. 'And it's not a touristy beach like the one at Ayr. But it'd be cool, all the same.'

'No, seriously, I'd love that.'

There's a rustling sound from Mouse's sleeping

bag, and he peers out, sleepy-eyed, over the top.

'Yeah, cool,' he says, yawning.

Finn looks embarrassed. 'Hey, thought you were asleep, little mate,' he says. 'Thing is, Mouse, I was thinking that maybe just Dizz and me would go to the beach. Take some time out, do teenage stuff, y'know?'

Mouse frowns. 'No,' he says. 'No, I don't know.'

Finn rakes a hand through his felted hair. 'Well, it's not really your kind of beach, Mouse,' he sighs. 'No ice cream, no tourists, nothing flashy. It's just dunes and mud and gullies and rocks. Pretty boring.'

'No, it sounds *great*,' Mouse argues.

Finn rolls his eyes. He's wavering. He doesn't like to hurt anyone's feelings, and he definitely doesn't want to hurt Mouse. 'Look, Mouse, little mate . . .' he begins.

'I think Tess needs you here, Mouse,' I say gently. 'Aren't you in charge of the bonfire? You have to make sure it's finished, show Niall how to edge it with rocks, get it started. Tess'll be relying on you.'

Mouse stares at me, his eyes huge. Then he looks at Finn. He's sitting up now, his hair sticking up in tufts. His lower lip trembles.

'You don't want me, do you?' he says.

'It's not that we don't want you . . .'

'You *don't*,' Mouse says. 'You think I'll get in the way. You think I'll spoil things. People always think that.'

Finn looks angry. 'No, Mouse, seriously. I just want to spend some time alone with Dizzy, OK? On my birthday,' he says. 'Is that too much to ask?'

'Don't *want* to go, anyway. Sounds rubbish.'

Mouse struggles out of his sleeping bag and dives for the rope-ladder. He drops down into the bushes and crashes off into the dark. Leggit crouches on the platform, whining, then leaps down to follow.

'OK,' sighs Finn. 'That went kind of wrong, didn't it?'

'Kind of.'

'Shall I go after him?'

'Better let him calm down.'

Finn is silent, staring out into the dark.

'I guess he'll get over it,' he says.

Mouse sulks all week.

On Friday morning, he tucks a king-size Mars bar under Finn's pillow and sneaks away.

'Think I'm forgiven?' Finn asks, showing me.

'Hope so.'

I give him the guitar strap, wrapped in tissue paper.

'Wow!' he says, stroking the embroidered patterns. 'Dizzy, it's amazing! I love it!' He unclips the old guitar strap and ties the new one on. He tries it for size, strums a few notes, does a little dance.

'Look, no hands! Oh, Dizz, this is cool.'

He puts down the guitar and for a minute I think he's going to hug me, but Mouse appears, and he gets hugged instead. 'Thanks for the choccy, little mate,' Finn says. 'My favourite.'

We pack towels and swimsuits and apples and peanut-butter sandwiches. Tess drives us to the bus stop and waves us off.

'Don't get into any trouble,' she says.

'Mu-um!' says Finn. 'As if!'

It feels weird without Mouse and Leggit. We sit side by side on the bus, fiddling with bus tickets, looking out of the window. Finn unwraps the birthday Mars bar, breaking it in half.

'Breakfast, Mouse-style,' he grins.

I laugh, and take a bite.

We get off at a road-end in the middle of nowhere, and walk down a steep, skinny lane. The sun warms our backs. I wish this summer would never end, but it's almost the end of August. It can't go on forever.

'Back to school, soon,' I say gloomily.

'Don't! I'm fourteen now,' Finn sulks. 'School gets serious. Revision, exams, acres of course-work.'

I think of green stripy ties in the grey Birmingham drizzle, the boiled cabbage and disinfectant smell of school corridors.

'I don't want to go back.'

To my old school, my old life, my old self.

'I know. Wish you didn't have to. You could come to my school, maybe.'

'Maybe,' I shrug, but both of us know it's not going to happen. Tess is already pretty stressy about being left with Mouse and me. The day before yesterday she wrote to Dad, and she's been in touch with the social services in London, too, trying to find out about Mouse's mum.

'D'you like school?' I ask Finn.

'It's OK,' he shrugs. 'It's just one of those things you have to get through. You just find a way of making it work for you.'

'Did you ever get picked on?' I ask.

'Sure, in Year Seven,' Finn admits. 'I had long hair – it wasn't dreaded, then – and Niall's old hand-me-down uniform. I was always getting hauled up to play piano in assembly. *So* embarrassing. There was this group of older lads – they couldn't work out if I was a wuss or a weirdo. They used to knock into me in the dinner queue, hack me at football, push me on the stairwells. Call me names and stuff.'

Finn frowns, remembering.

'What did you do?'

'I got into a scrap in the middle of a footy match, gave one kid a black eye. I got suspended for a week. They never touched me after that.'

'You were suspended!' I cry, outraged. 'Didn't you explain? Didn't you tell them about the bullying?'

'Didn't see the point,' Finn shrugs.

'You're crazy,' I scold him. 'What did Tess say?'

'She wasn't exactly overjoyed.'

We climb a farm gate and trail up across a

steeply sloping field. The farmer has just cut the grass for hay and rolled it into bales. It smells like heaven.

'It's not so bad now,' Finn says. 'My music teacher introduced me to this kid Jon, who's really into drumming. We worked out that we liked the same music, so we started jamming together. My mate Danny joined in on bass guitar, and we had a band. Spider Pie. We get to play at end-of-term concerts, that sort of thing. We're kind of louder and janglier than the teachers like, but it's better than hammering out the tune for 'Go Tell it on the Mountain' in assembly every week, y'know?'

'I know. I'll watch out for you on the Kerrang! channel.'

'Do that!'

Finn stops to pick a thorn out of his foot.

'D'you wear shoes to school?' I ask.

Finn raises an eyebrow. 'Of course I do. What d'you take me for, a rebel or something?'

'Something,' I laugh. 'I just can't imagine you in Nike trainers and a stripy tie.'

'Trainers? Who said anything about trainers? My school shoes are sixteen-hole Doc Martens with lime-green and black striped bootlaces. And I *always* wear my tie. Round my wrist – or to tie my hair back.'

I laugh, trying to imagine.

We're almost at the top of the hill now. I'm hot and tired. 'Where is this beach?' I ask. 'Outer Mongolia?'

'Patience,' Finn says. 'And remember what I said to Mouse. Don't expect anything fancy.'

We climb up over the brow of the hill and there it is, at the foot of the slope. A wide, shimmering curve of turquoise water, a streak of sludge-coloured mud, a jigsaw of gullies and rock pools.

'Wow.'

It's not pretty, but it's a beach – and we have it all to ourselves.

'Race ya!' Finn shouts, and we're flying down the hillside, arms spread wide, hair streaming out behind us. We crash into the wall that borders the field and clamber over, breathless. The grass thins out, turns scruffy, then gives way to big rocks and patches of mud.

I take off my trainers and pick my way over the stones. Finn is way ahead, balancing on slabs of slimy stone and peering into rock pools crusted with barnacles. When I catch up, he has his feet in the water, a pale golden crab edging sideways over his toes.

'Eeew!' I squeal.

'It tickles!'

'Poor crab,' I sympathize.

'Cheek!' Finn nudges me and I slip, one foot

landing in the pool next to his. I yelp. The water is freezing, and I pull my foot out. The crab darts away under a rock.

'You scared it,' Finn says.

'*You* scared it.'

Finn pulls a face, and I pull one back, laughing. He goes on looking at me for way too long, and I have to look away before I do anything sad and dorky, like blush.

We wade out along the gullies and channels, kick our way along the water's edge.

'It's *cold*!' I screech.

'It's gorgeous! Don't be so chicken!'

We push and shove and splash each other, until at last we're not fighting so much as holding hands. Finn's palm feels big and rough and warm, wrapped round mine. We splash through the cool, clean water, feet sinking into soft mud, toes scraping against sharp-ridged shells. Long scarves of seaweed tangle round our ankles like fine, emerald hair.

'D'you ever wish you could just stop time?' Finn asks. 'Keep things frozen, the way they are?'

'Sure,' I whisper. 'Before real life gets in the way again.'

He squeezes my fingers, and we break apart. Suddenly, I can breathe again.

'Let's beachcomb,' I say. 'Find something to take back for Mouse.'

We walk up to the tideline and scour the ribbon of driftwood and rubbish for hidden treasures. We rescue a clutch of long, white feathers, nuggets of dusty, jewel-bright seaglass and the shell of a giant crab, complete with claws.

'He'll love these,' Finn says, packing them carefully away inside his rucksack. 'Y'know, with Mouse, it's kind of like having a little brother all of a sudden. I like it!'

'I know. Me, too. It's like we're a family, somehow, the three of us.'

Finn frowns, kicking at a tangle of frayed blue rope, an empty plastic pop bottle. 'I don't want to be your brother,' he says darkly. 'I don't feel that way. Not like your *brother*.'

'I know.'

And I do, suddenly. In the family we've invented, Finn and me are *not* brother and sister. His hand snakes out to capture mine again, and I don't pull away. We walk on.

Round the tip of a jutting headland, we find a tiny, sheltered cove of soft golden sand. Beyond, the fields slope upwards, green meadows scattered with wildflowers. It's a tiny, secret beach, half-hidden between the hills.

'Hey!' Finn shouts, delighted. 'I don't remember this. It's amazing!'

'It's a magic birthday beach,' I tell him. 'Just here for one day. At midnight it disappears.'

We drop our backpacks and run out across the hot sand. The grains stick to our muddy feet, spray out behind us. Finn stretches his arms wide, whirls round a couple of times. He spins in the soft sand, arms outstretched, until he keels over and collapses. He looks up at me, grinning.

'D'you remember when we were little?' he asks, breathless. 'We used to spin round and round till we fell, and we called it the Dizzy Game. Remember?'

'I think so . . .'

I know the Dizzy Game, of course I do, from sunny days on the school field with Sasha and Sara and Jade. I just didn't realize it came from a time *before* school, when Finn and I were first friends.

If Finn isn't too shy to hurl himself round in circles until he staggers, screaming, and crashes into the sand, then I'm not. I spread my arms and turn, slowly at first, then faster and faster, out of control. The world spins away and my feet lose their hold on the earth and I'm squealing, staggering, stumbling.

Then the ground shifts and comes up to slap my back, my head. I lie in the soft, golden sand as the world spins round me, and I remember why I used to love this game. It makes everything go away, until there's just you, your head reeling, your heart thumping. Real life churns on, the earth tilts, the sky dips.

I grab handfuls of sand to get a hold of myself, but the grains run away through my fingers. The hot sun presses me down. A hand brushes past my outstretched fingers, weaves between them. Finn. We lie still for a few minutes, fingertips touching, waiting for the world to stop.

Then Finn is struggling upright, dragging me with him. I stumble against him, laughing, and his hands cup my face. He looks at me for a long moment, and then he's kissing me.

It's not like I imagined. His lips taste of salt and sand and happiness. They're soft, so soft. We break apart and we can't stop staring at each other, wide-eyed. He brushes sand from my cheek, my hair.

The world keeps on spinning, with or without the Dizzy Game.

The bus drops us off at six, and we hear the music as we turn into the lane, see the lanterns twinkling up ahead. There's a smell of wood smoke and barbecued tofu.

As we push open the gate, Leggit leaps forwards. Someone's made her a collar of willow and flowers, and she jumps up at us, trailing ribbons and licking the salt from our skin.

'Finn! Dizz!' Mouse calls out from the tree house.

'Hey, Mouse! We did some beachcombing for you.'

Mouse is wriggling down the rope-ladder, bounding towards us through the flowers. He watches as Finn unwraps the parcel of treasure, reaching out to touch the soft white feathers, the seaglass, the crab shell.

'Cool,' he breathes. 'Will you take me, next time?'

'Sure,' I tell him. 'Next time.'

'We missed you, little mate,' Finn says.

'Did you have your Mars bar?'

'Long gone, Mouse. But much appreciated. The best prezzie ever.'

Mouse flashes us a smile. 'The best is yet to come,' he tells us. 'Just you wait and see!'

Then Tess is calling us, and Finn's gran, and Niall, and Mouse melts into the background, eyes bright, smiling his secret smile. The barbie is ready, and we stack our plates high with charred sweetcorn, tofu burgers, veggie kebabs. Someone's brought the CD player and speakers outside, and Niall removes a Bob Dylan CD, feeding it instead with Finn's favourite clashy, trashy nu-metal sounds.

Finn's opening presents now – a new hoodie, a pair of baggy jeans, a couple of piano music books, a beautiful, handpainted bodhrán drum. It's like a big, wide tambourine with weird Celtic dragons painted on the skin. Finn holds it flat against his body, flicking the drumstick over it in a fast, furious beat.

We sit round the bonfire and eat and laugh and talk. It gets dark, and Finn pulls on his hoodie, while Tess hands round sparklers. I dip mine into the bonfire flame and watch it fizz, then write *Dizzy + Finn* into the darkness, so fast that nobody could ever know. Except Finn, who catches my eye and draws a heart in the air between us.

Mouse tries juggling the sparklers, but Tess says it's dangerous and threatens to take them away. Instead, Mouse puts on a juggling show with three velvet beanbags, tossing them higher and higher in the bonfire's flickering light. He throws them at Niall, who flings them back in a quick volley. Mouse doesn't drop a single throw.

'*Could* have done it with fire,' he says, to prove a point.

'Maybe,' I tell him. 'But I'm glad you didn't. Nothing could have been better than this, Mouse.'

'Think so? *That* was nothing. You'll see.'

I pull a face, then turn back to the bonfire. I notice Finn's BMX ramp pulled up way too close to the edge of it, flames licking the wood. I kick it, managing to knock it a few inches backwards. 'It's a bit black around the edges,' I shout to Finn, who shrugs. It's only a home-made thing, so I guess it doesn't matter.

'Mouse again,' Tess sighs. 'He was riding the BMX up and over the bonfire, earlier, again and again. Before it was lit, obviously!'

'He's getting pretty good!'

'Sure,' Tess says. 'He's got a skill, definitely. Like with the juggling. And he'll try anything – he just doesn't seem to get scared at all.'

'Maybe,' says Finn, joining us. 'Or maybe he's just scared of different things.'

'Maybe. Better go get that cake organized, anyhow,' Tess says.

A minute later she's in the cottage doorway, shouting for Niall. 'Quick! Niall! That wretched goat's got loose again, it's in the kitchen! Give us a hand!'

Niall runs off towards the house.

'Wonder if she was in time to save the cake?' Finn muses. 'Last time Cedric got in the house, he ate a bowl of ice cream, my Year Eight physics textbook and Gran's cardigan. Scary.'

Finn's gran is sitting on a log at the other side of the bonfire. She looks tired, dreamy. She doesn't notice when Finn edges closer to me, when his hand slides over mine. 'Today was brilliant,' he whispers into my hair.

I let my hair fall forwards to hide my flaming cheeks. I can't think of anything to say. Suddenly, typically, the CD player stops and Niall isn't there to keep it fed with discs, to plug the long, heavy silence.

'Hey!'

We both jump.

'Watch me!'

Mouse is behind us on the grass, waving, grinning, a tiny, skinny figure astride Finn's BMX.

Something looks odd about it. Then I realize – there are sparklers stuck all round the wheel rims of the bike, jutting their fuzzy, crackling fire into the clear night air.

'Looks cool, Mouse,' Finn starts to say, but the words die on his lips as Mouse pedals forwards, hammering down the slope and across the grass. The sparklers leave a trail of silver as the wheels spin.

He's heading straight for the ramp, the bonfire. He's been practising all day, hasn't he? Before the bonfire was lit, obviously. Only there's no obviously with Mouse. There never has been.

*That was nothing. You'll see.*

I'm starting to see, Mouse. I am.

I open my mouth to scream, but it feels like it's full of sand. No sound comes. Finn's gran is on her feet on the other side of the bonfire, her face white. Leggit starts to whine.

Mouse flies straight at the ramp, up and into the bonfire. The bike hovers, high above the flames, and Mouse tries for a bar spin. He's going to make it. He spins the handlebars, and the wheel turns quickly. And then it stops, and the bike is dropping, down into the fire.

'There's a branch in the wheel!' Finn gasps.

Mouse is pushing himself away from the bike, leaping away from the flames. He can still make it.

Then the bike is gone, and Mouse falls after it, down into the bonfire.

And into the silence of the stopped CD player comes his scream, loud and thin and ugly.

It goes on and on and on.

Everything happens slowly, then everything happens fast.

Finn pulls up the hood of his jacket, drags the sleeves down over his hands and runs into the bonfire. He claws at the burning branches, hauls the bike to one side. And then he's falling backwards on to the grass, with Mouse in his arms.

Tiny flames curl all along Mouse's jeans, his sweatshirt, but Finn rolls him over and over, holding him close. He smothers the flames with his own body, and then he lets go, rolls away.

Mouse is still, silent.

Finn's gran is there suddenly, dragging the hosepipe. She pours water over Mouse's blackened clothing, dousing him, soaking him. His little body jerks and shudders.

'*Don't!*' I yell at her. 'It's hurting him! Are you meant to do that?'

'Get Tess,' she says to me. 'Tell her to call an ambulance.'

I hesitate. There's a stink of burning rubber from the bike, and the smell of burned fabric, and something worse. It could be hair, or skin.

'*Quickly!*' screams Finn's gran, and because I've never heard her raise her voice before, I push back my terror and run up to the house.

Tess appears in the doorway with a huge sponge cake studded with lit candles. Behind her, in the hall, Niall is scuffling with Cedric.

'Isn't it great?' Tess beams. 'D'you think he'll like it? Dizzy? What's the matter, Dizz?'

'The bonfire – Mouse fell – Finn – we need an ambulance . . .'

Then the stench from the bonfire fills my nostrils again, and I turn away into the bushes and retch.

Tess runs down to the bonfire, dropping the cake on to the path. Niall rings for the ambulance, then puts an arm round my shoulders and leads me back down to the others.

Mouse lies curled on the grass, his face white, his eyelids flickering. Finn's gran kneels beside him, offering sips of water. Leggit skulks nearby, cringing and whining. She pushes Mouse with her long wolf's muzzle, her big pink tongue, and his hand uncurls to touch her.

He doesn't look too bad. Until he turns his head, and I see what the fire has really done. I turn away, sickened.

Finn lies a few feet away, hunched over, Tess bathing his feet and legs with a rag soaked in water. Then I realize that the rag is a piece of her skirt, torn roughly from the rest.

'Oh, Finn, Finn,' she whispers. 'Your poor feet.'

I can't look at Finn's feet, his beautiful, bare feet that ran through white-hot embers and leaping flames to rescue Mouse. Instead I look at his face, scrunched up in pain, wet with tears.

There's a small, dark shape on the grass at the bonfire's edge. An old toy mouse, slightly blackened now. I pick it up, my fingers shaking.

The ambulance takes Mouse and Finn and Tess, and Finn's gran takes the car with Niall and me. We drive through the night and end up in the Specialist Burns Unit of a big hospital, miles away. We sit in a corridor that reeks of bleach and fear, waiting for news. Tess is hollow-eyed, grey with pain.

'It's my fault,' she whispers. 'I should have *known*. All day he was practising with that BMX, flying up the ramp, leaping the bonfire. I should have known. I should have guessed.'

'How could you?' Niall soothes. 'It was a crazy thing to do.'

'His face,' Tess breathes. 'His little face, all down one side. And Finn's feet. Oh, God, how many times have I told him to wear shoes?'

'Mum, don't,' Niall says. 'It's nobody's fault.'

But it is, of course.

OK, Mouse was crazy to try the jump. It was a risk, but it nearly came off. If he hadn't tried the bar spin, if the front wheel hadn't tangled with that branch . . .

If I hadn't kicked the ramp back.

All day he practised, getting everything perfect. And I moved the ramp.

It was *my* fault. I choke back another wave of nausea and let the tears fall. My eyes sting, like they're full of grit.

After what feels like a hundred years or so, an Asian doctor and a little blonde nurse come out to talk to Tess.

'Will they be OK?' she asks, hanging on to the doctor's arm. 'How does it look? Will they . . .?'

'They're comfortable,' the doctor says. 'The little boy has some partial and some full-thickness burns to the head, shoulder and hands, and less severe damage to the chest and back. He will recover, but there'll be scarring. Perhaps, later, we can do some cosmetic work, help to lessen the impact.'

'And Finn?'

'Some damage to the hands and wrists, but nothing serious. It's his feet we're concerned about. It's too soon to say how well things will heal, but again, there will certainly be scarring.'

'But they'll be OK?' Tess asks again. 'Won't they?'

The nurse smiles sadly. 'Yes, Mrs Campbell, they'll be OK. Now . . . is there anyone I can call for you? How about the boys' father?'

'Oh, no, we're not together any more,' Tess murmurs. 'And Mouse's dad's in India. Although I suppose perhaps his mum should know . . .'

The doctor frowns. 'The littlest boy . . . he's not yours?' he asks slowly.

'No, no, he was just staying . . . for a while . . .'

'And his dad is abroad? Where is his mum?'

'She's ill,' Finn's gran says. 'She's in London, somewhere, in a clinic. My daughter's been helping out.'

'I see. And what relation, exactly, are you both to the little boy?'

'Well,' flounders Tess. 'No *relation*, exactly.'

'I see.'

'Somebody had to look after them,' Finn's gran says anxiously.

'*Them?*' says the nurse.

'Well, you know, Mouse and Dizzy.'

The doctor looks at Tess, then me. 'Dizzy,' he

says. 'The sister of the little boy who fell in the fire?'

'Yes,' I say.

'No,' Tess corrects. 'Not exactly. She's just staying with us. Her mum is in India, her dad's in Birmingham.'

'I see.'

They turn away.

'Social services,' the nurse whispers, when she thinks we're out of earshot.

A little while later, they lead us through to see Finn and Mouse. They're sleeping, sedated, the nurse says. Finn looks OK, but looking at Mouse is like seeing a TV report from a war zone. Cling film stuff swathes one side of his face, hides his hands. I reach into my pocket for the skanky toy mouse, tuck it in under the covers, softly.

It's just past nine in the morning when we get back to Bramble Cottage. The sun streaks through the apple-tree branches, still strung with jam-jar lanterns, long since dead. The bonfire still smoulders on the grass, a low mound of grey ash and charred logs. The blackened skeleton of the BMX lies half-in, half-out of the embers.

On the path, a broken china plate marks where Tess dropped Finn's birthday cake. There's no trace of the sponge, jam, cream or candles.

'Goat probably had it,' says Niall. 'Lucky thing.'

The cottage door stands open, the way we left it. The tabby cat lies stretched out in the hallway, basking in a patch of sun.

'Bed,' Tess says wearily. 'All of us, and in the house, Dizzy, not the tree house. We need some rest if we're going to see the boys later on.'

'OK.'

Inside the cottage the phone begins to ring, and Tess wanders off to get it.

'Pot of chamomile tea?' Finn's gran suggests. 'Settle us down?'

We can hear Tess talking in the other room.

'You don't think it could be the hospital?' I ask.

'No, no. Stop worrying,' says Niall.

But when Tess comes into the kitchen, our eyes swivel to her. She tries to fix her face into a happy shape, but it doesn't quite come off.

'Dizzy . . .' she says slowly. 'That was your dad.'

The doorbell rings and rings, somewhere far away. It hauls me out of sleep and I sit up, wearily, rubbing my eyes. It rings again.

Sunlight streams in through thin red curtains, and the bedside clock says just before midday. The walls are covered in black-and-white posters of sulky LA punk bands, and a pair of Doc Martens with lime-green stripy laces sit under the desk. Finn's room.

The doorbell rings again, and I run across the landing, down the stairs. I see dark shadows through the front door's coloured glass.

I open the door, still rubbing my eyes.

'Dad!'

I fling myself at him, and he lifts me right up off the ground like he used to when I was little, swinging me round and round. We come back down to earth, hanging on tighter than ever. I bury my face in his neck and there's a funny, snuffly sound that means he's either laughing or crying.

I don't care which. He's here.

We don't let go, not for a long time. When we move apart, there's a wet patch on my hair where it lay against his cheek, and his eyes are damp and blurry, just like mine.

Dad looks different, somehow. His dark hair is grey at the temples, his face kind of grey and sad. There are lines etched across his forehead that never used to be there. It's like I haven't seen him for ten years, not ten weeks.

'You came,' I say, and my voice comes out all husky and ragged. 'At last, you came!'

A flash of what looks like pain crosses Dad's face. 'Oh, Dizzy,' he says sadly. 'Of course I did.'

Behind him, looking neat and pretty and wonderfully familiar in a blue top and embroidered jeans, is Lucy. She looks uncertain, anxious, but her lips twitch into a nervous smile. Over her shoulder I see the blue Mini pulled up on the driveway. Cedric is hovering by the front wheel, sniffing thoughtfully.

'Lucy,' I say.

'Dizz.'

She hugs me, just a quick, light hug. I hug her back. Behind me, Tess is coming down the stairs, a crocheted shawl wrapped round her nightie.

'Pete,' she says. 'Long time no see. Look, come

in, both of you. Just let me call the hospital, then we'll talk. Get to the bottom of this mess.'

I take them through to the kitchen, put the kettle on.

'How is – Finn, is it? Tess's son?' Dad asks. 'And the other little boy? How did it happen?'

I turn away. 'It was Finn's birthday. Mouse was showing off, trying to impress us. He tried a BMX jump right over the bonfire, but one of the wheels got tangled and he fell in. Finn pulled him out.'

'How awful,' says Lucy.

Dad nods, a hand over his mouth, forehead creased. He's thinking that it could have been me.

'Someone moved the ramp,' I say into the silence. 'That's why he didn't make it. He had it all worked out, but someone moved the ramp.'

Dad looks at me. 'No, no, Dizzy,' he says slowly. 'It was a dangerous thing to do, that's all. If it hadn't been the ramp, it'd have been something else.'

'He should have checked it,' says Lucy.

'He's only seven.'

'Ah, Dizz.'

Tess sweeps into the room, trailing the shawl.

'So?' Dad asks. 'How are they? Any news?'

'Better,' she admits. 'They're resting. We can visit later.'

Tess sits down, heavily. 'Anyway, Pete, um . . . Lucy? It's good to see you. Find us OK?'

Dad just stares. '*Find* you OK?' he says, shakily. 'Not really, no. It's taken ten weeks, hasn't it? This whole thing has been a nightmare. Not one word until your letter.'

'I had no idea, Pete,' Tess says. 'Believe me, until you rang this morning I really had no idea.'

I put three mugs of herb tea and an apple juice on the tabletop.

'You knew I was here, though, right?' I say. 'Storm said she'd keep you posted.'

Dad closes his eyes, takes a couple of deep breaths.

'Keep me posted?' he says at last. 'That's a joke, Dizzy. I've been looking for you since the day after your birthday, the day you took off. Nine weeks and six days. I can tell you the hours, the minutes, the seconds, too. I thought I'd never see you again.'

'Sit down, Dizzy,' Tess says gently.

I sit.

'It looks like Storm wasn't totally upfront with you when she said she'd asked your dad about this holiday . . .'

'Holiday!' Dad rasps. 'Kidnap, I call it! Don't defend her, Tess. Storm is in big trouble, this time. She's gone too far. Too far.'

'But you *knew* I was coming,' I argue. 'Storm said you were fine with it. And I told you myself, that morning, when I was saying goodbye . . .'

Dad drops his head into his hands. 'No, Dizz,' he says sadly. '*No*, you didn't. I was pretty hung-over, but I know I'd have remembered if you told me you were running away with your mum for the summer. I . . . I thought you were going to school . . .'

Lucy reaches a hand out to cover mine. 'He started to worry when you didn't come home that afternoon,' she says. 'He rang Jade and Sara and Sasha, but of course they hadn't seen you. Then we went to the police . . .'

The *police*? My heart is thumping.

*Storm, Storm, what have you done?*

The story unravels. The police talked to Dad, decided that it was a pretty sure thing I was with my mum. They put me on the Missing Persons list, but they didn't do much about tracking me down. I was with family, they said. It wasn't a priority.

Lucy drove Dad to Wales in the blue Mini and they searched every festival, every open-air concert, every scrap of countryside.

'I wasn't in Wales,' I tell them. 'I was never in Wales. It was *Scotland*.'

'Right,' Dad sighs. 'Clever girl, Storm. Later on,

the police told us that a traveller girl meeting your description had been picked up for shoplifting in Ayr. By the time they realized and went back to look, she – you? – had gone.'

'It *was* me,' I tell him. 'It was. But I wasn't shoplifting.'

'Unreal,' Tess says. 'All that fuss about moving on, packing up in the middle of the night. Storm *knew*.'

Dad shrugs. 'We drove up to Scotland and searched ourselves, but nobody had heard of you, or Storm. Or if they did, they weren't saying.'

'Did you ring, one day?' Lucy asks suddenly. 'Then hang up?'

I nod, red-faced. 'I don't know why. I was scared. I got confused. I'm sorry.'

Lucy looks at me for a long time. She knows why I hung up. Because I was jealous, hurt, stupid. But if she can read my mind, she must know how sorry I am. Mustn't she?

'Doesn't matter, now,' she says softly. 'We've found you.'

'I sent postcards,' I remember suddenly. 'Five postcards. Didn't you get them?'

Dad's eyes widen. 'No, not one. Are you sure you sent them?'

I'm silent. I wrote them, and, each time, I handed them to Storm. *Let me add my own little message*, she used to say. Or, *I'll post it when I'm in town. No trouble.*

'I gave them to Storm.'

Dad drains his coffee mug and puts it down, wearily. 'So,' he says. 'Where is your mother? Where *is* Storm?'

Tess stands up, wrapping the shawl tightly round herself. 'When I sent the letter, I kind of assumed you knew,' she says. 'And then, when you rang this morning, I realized things were all wrong, but I just didn't know how to tell you.'

'Tell me *what*?'

'It's Mum,' I say. 'She's not here any more. Not for three, four weeks. She's gone to India.'

28

We stay on at the cottage for a while. Each day, I go to see Finn and Mouse in hospital. I get so I don't flinch when I see the shiny patches on Finn's feet, the shimmery cling-film dressings on Mouse's head and hands and shoulders.

Finn is well enough to sit in a wheelchair and scoosh along the corridor to see Mouse. His feet are still painful, but they're healing well.

'Guess I won't go barefoot in summer, any more,' he says.

'Guess not.'

Mouse is chirpier than you'd expect.

'I nearly made it, didn't I?' he says one visiting time. 'It was a pretty good jump, wasn't it?'

'Mouse! You could have been killed!'

'Nah,' he says. 'Next time, I'll do it for sure.'

'No next time, Mouse,' I tell him gently.

'No?'

'No,' Finn says sternly. 'No way.'

Mouse shrugs.

I take a deep breath and tell Mouse about moving the ramp. 'It's my fault, isn't it?' I ask him. 'My fault it went wrong?'

'How far did you kick the ramp?'

'Not far, it was heavy. A few inches?' I spread my fingers, guessing at the distance.

Mouse shakes his head sadly. 'Shouldn't have made any difference,' he says. 'It was a perfect jump. It was just that branch that got in the way. Maybe I shouldn't have tried the bar spin?'

'Maybe you shouldn't have tried any of it!'

Mouse grins. 'It was for you,' he says. 'For you and Finn.'

Finn reaches out and tweaks his ear, the one that isn't cocooned in cling film. The one that isn't burnt. 'I know, Mouse,' he says. 'I know, little mate.'

'I nearly made it,' Mouse says again.

'Yeah, you nearly did.'

But nearly isn't good enough.

A nurse comes to change the dressings, and we glimpse patches of weird, puckered skin on Mouse's neck and cheek and ear and hands and shoulders. The nurse says the scarring will fade, but it won't go away. Mouse looks in the mirror and pulls a face. He doesn't look too bothered.

The whole time Mouse is in hospital, the nurses

and social workers are trying to work out what to do with him. They contact the detox clinic in London. The doctors there say his mum is getting better, but she's still not well enough to look after him. With difficulty, they get a message to Zak in Goa. He rings the hospital and speaks to the doctors, rings the social services and speaks to Mouse's case worker. Finally he rings the cottage and speaks to Tess.

Tess waves us through to the living room and puts the call on speakerphone, so we can hear what he says. We watch as she goes over things one more time for Zak.

'I'm so sorry it happened,' she says. 'We're all sorry. The doctors say he's doing well.'

Things are at a difficult stage with the healing centre, Zak says. There's so much work still to be done to get it up and running, and Josh is relying on him. Coming back to England is kind of awkward right now.

'Couldn't Mouse just stay with you a bit longer?' Zak asks.

Tess has to explain about the social workers. 'They're not all that happy about the situation,' she says. 'I've said he can stay here, of course I have. But it's not that simple. Zak, if you don't come back and get him, I think they might take him into care.'

'No, no, they won't do that, surely,' says Zak.

We lean against the sofa, watching Tess.

'I think that they will,' she tells him.

Zak is silent for a while.

'I suppose he could come out here,' he says at last, grudgingly. 'Only there's nobody to watch out for him, really. I'd just worry about him being safe. Unless Dizzy could come out to keep an eye on him?'

Dad grabs the phone from Tess. 'Dizzy *can't*,' he says crisply. 'Dizzy has school to go to, a life to live. She can't go chasing to the other side of the world to babysit your son. He's *your* responsibility, poor little kid. Can you put Storm on the line?'

'Storm can't come to the phone right now.'

'No, I *bet* she can't.'

Dad hands the receiver back to Tess, trembling with anger.

Zak starts asking whether Amber and Carl have paid up for the tepee yet. Money's a bit tight in Goa, he says. Could Tess chase up the cash for him?

Tess stares at the telephone, speechless.

'Who is this creep, anyway?' Dad asks out loud.

'Hello? Tess?' Zak is saying. 'About the money. Is anyone there?'

'Hi, Zak?' Tess says. 'I have to go now. Give my love to Storm, and tell her Dizzy's safe with her dad again. And, Zak, give Mouse a call at the hospital, yeah? He'd love to hear from you. OK?'

She puts the phone down, and rests her head in her hands.

'Poor Mouse,' says Finn's gran. 'D'you think he'll ring?'

'Maybe,' says Tess.

He doesn't, of course.

Finn's out of hospital first, but I'm well away by then, back in the drizzle and gloom of Birmingham.

We keep in touch, with letters and phone calls. Tess and Finn see Mouse just about every day. They say the doctors are pleased with his progress, but it's November before he's finally discharged. A social worker is taking him to London, to a foster family near the clinic where his mum is staying. He'll get to visit, maybe, when she's a bit better.

Dad and I travel up north to say goodbye. Tess and Finn meet us at the railway station, and we drive to the hospital together through the thin November sunshine.

Mouse is waiting for us in the hospital foyer, his new social worker standing guard. We wave and hug and then stand around, awkward and embarrassed, not wanting to say goodbye.

Mouse is clean and neat, but the smile has gone. His cheeky, flashing eyes are dull and quiet, his face closed, sullen. The burns are way better, and his hair has grown back to a stubbly crew cut. It looks weird, like the clothes they've given him to wear, all trackies and sporty, label stuff.

'Can we have some time?' Tess asks the social worker. 'On our own?'

The social worker, a young man with gold-rimmed specs and a toothy grin, says he'll wait. 'Not too long, mind. It's a long drive to London, hey Mouse?'

Mouse scowls. A *very* long drive, I think.

We go outside, the social worker trailing at a distance. He finds a bench and sits down, watching us. Dad hangs back too, while Tess, Finn and I walk out across the grass with Mouse.

'Hang on, Mouse,' Finn says suddenly. 'Got a surprise for you!'

He runs off towards the car park, still limping a little.

'We'll miss you,' Tess says into the silence. 'We'll ring, see how you're settling in.'

Mouse looks away.

'It's not for long,' she says brightly. 'Your mum will be well enough to look after you, soon. And you'll be living nearby, they'll take you to visit her. That'll be good, won't it?'

Mouse kicks at a stone, scuffing up some turf on the toe of his new trainers.

'I'll miss you,' I whisper.

His eyes snap up to mine, blazing. 'You promised,' he says, his lower lip quivering. 'You promised you'd look after me, you and Finn. You said you wouldn't let the bad people get me! You said!'

I fling my arms round him and hug him tight. 'I won't, I won't, I never will,' I tell him. 'I promise, Mouse, never!'

When we pull apart, he looks at me so sadly that I wonder if Mouse's 'bad people' really are the lowlifes and the thieves I imagined. Maybe not. Maybe it's not that simple. Maybe they're the people trying to help, like the nice social worker with the trendy specs and the wide grin, sitting on a bench with his newspaper.

'It'll be OK, Mouse,' I tell him.

He nods, trying for a smile, acting brave.

'They washed my mouse,' he says, holding out a pale, battered, unrecognizable toy. 'He's not the same any more. D'you want him?'

'Really?'

'Really. So you won't forget me.'

'Oh, Mouse, how could I?'

I take the toy mouse, anyway. It's still kind of scorched all down one side, from the bonfire.

'Hey, watch out!'

We turn just in time to see Leggit racing towards us, a streak of black and white, tail waving like a flag. She circles Mouse, yelping wildly, then leaps up and topples him on to the grass, licking his face, making muddy pawprints on his new grey sweatshirt.

'Leggit! Bad girl! Hey, hey!' Mouse laughs, and he hugs her, ruffling her raggedy fur, patting her skinny ribs. He hangs on for ages, hiding his face in her fur, and when he comes up for air, his cheeks are streaked with tears.

'Got something in my eye,' he says gruffly.

'Yeah, I know, little mate,' Finn says, dragging a sleeve across his face. 'Me, too.'

So I'm back in the land of stripy school ties and maths tests and shared Cokes, of hot showers and takeaway pizzas and Sky TV. I walk around the flat barefoot, letting my toes sink into the soft carpet, wishing it was cool grass, hot sand, scratchy shells. I open windows and breathe in exhaust fumes, pollution, the thump of a ghetto blaster from across the road.

After Christmas, Lucy moves into the flat. I don't mind as much as I thought I would.

She fills the bathroom with fruity shower gels and scented candles and soap that smells like coconut ice. When Dad's working late in the workshop, we watch slushy films and eat toffee popcorn and do each other's hair. The models he makes of elves and fairies and sad-faced mermaids all start to look a bit like Lucy. It's OK.

Jade and Sara and Sasha pump me for information about Finn.

'Are you in love?' Sasha wants to know. 'Or was it just a crush?'

I laugh. 'Don't know about love. It's just – he's my best friend. Apart from you guys, of course!'

Or maybe even including.

'Did you kiss him?' Jade demands.

'Like I'm gonna tell *you* that!'

'You did! She did!' Sara squeals, and they collapse in hysterics, making kissy-kissy noises and fluttering their lashes.

One day, when I'm feeling brave, I show them the pictures I took with the camera Lucy gave me. There's Tess, in a flower crown, looking up from the Calor gas stove outside the tent. There's Zak, juggling batons in the veggie patch at Bramble Cottage, and Storm, her face a swirl of pink and purple face paint, sticking her tongue out at the camera.

And there's Finn, cradling my guitar on the sand at Ayr beach; Finn sitting by the waterfall; Finn's face, close-up and crusted with sand, his eyes the same colour as the turquoise ocean.

'He's cool,' Jade says. 'Weird, but cool.'

'Amazing eyes,' Sara breathes.

'And hair,' says Sasha. 'I wonder if he'll be famous one day? And you can say you knew him.'

When we get to the last photo, Mouse and

Leggit cuddled up in the tree house, the breath catches in my throat.

'Funny little kid,' says Jade.

'Cute,' says Sasha, not meaning it.

Sara, who knows how I feel about Mouse, squeezes my arm. 'He's OK, Dizz,' she tells me. 'You said so yourself. Maybe you'll get to go down and see him next year?'

'Maybe.'

Mouse has settled in really well with his new foster parents. He sees his real mum most weekends. She's out of the clinic now, and off the drugs, but she's not ready to look after Mouse again, not yet. I wonder how he feels about that? I wonder if he still has nightmares, cries in his sleep? It's not the kind of thing you can ask on the phone.

He's going to school and learning to read and write, anyway.

'Still practising your juggling?' I asked, last time I called. 'And the BMX stunts?'

There was a silence.

'I've got a GameBoy,' he said uncertainly.

'Oh. Right. That's great, Mouse.'

'Does Leggit miss me?' he asked then, all in a rush.

'Oh, Mouse, of course she does. Who's gonna feed her Mars bars and cold chips when you're not around? She misses you every day. We all do.'

Sometimes, every couple of months, I get a little parcel from Mouse, addressed to me in his foster mum's neat, sloping handwriting – a Mars bar, sometimes squashed, sometimes not. I never really know if it's for me or for Leggit, so we share it, half each.

Leggit lives with us, now.

Tess couldn't keep her because of the way she chased the goat and the cat and the chickens, the way she raced circuits round the garden, crashing through the flower beds, tearing up the lettuce plants. 'I will if I have to, of course, but . . .'

'Why should you?' Dad had argued. 'Storm should have thought. All her life she's left a trail of hurt and mess behind her.'

'Shhh,' Tess said, looking at me. Like it was something I didn't already know.

'Will Leggit have to go to the dog's home?' I asked Dad.

'No,' he'd said firmly. 'No way. Leggit's coming home with us.'

She did.

The spiky, excitable festival dog who stole your chips and knocked you over with her tail is gone forever. Leggit gets brushed every day, so her hair is soft and clean and fluffy. She wears a red leather collar and walks on a lead without pulling. She has two big meals and never scrounges in between.

Dad takes her to dog-training classes, and now she can sit, lie, stay, walk to heel.

She is a reformed character. Just occasionally, when she's lying upside down on the white, fluffy rug by the fire, her legs in the air, I think I catch a glimpse of her wicked, wolfish side. Maybe, when we visit Finn and Tess this summer, it'll surface again.

We're all going, Dad and Lucy and Leggit and me. We've tried to arrange for Mouse to come out, too, but his foster parents aren't too keen. I guess I can see their point of view. They probably think it's some mad hippy commune where kids run wild and dangerous accidents lurk round every corner. How could you ever explain to them that it's the one place Mouse was truly happy?

Dad and Lucy have bought a tent specially – a big, fancy one with two bedrooms and a flashy porch at the front. We're going as soon as school is over, and that's not long, now.

Tomorrow is my birthday.

We're changing the tradition – we're going out for a meal, Dad and Lucy and me, then on to the multiplex to see a film. Things evolve, Dad says. They can't stay the same forever, they change the same way we do.

My room is different, too – the pinboard shrine full of treasures is gone. I packed away the doll, the hat, the postcards. I still have them, but I don't have them on show. I wrapped up the dream-catcher and sent it to Mouse. I reckon he needs all the help he can get, these days.

Now, my pinboard holds the photo of Finn with turquoise eyes, the snap of Mouse and Leggit in the tree house, a whole strip of Jade and Sasha and Sara and me, pulling scary faces, taken at a photo booth in town. Also skewered on are a Mars bar wrapper, a lime-green and black bootlace, a broken daisy chain, a small, faded, slightly toasted toy mouse. Bits of my life, things that make me smile.

A handful of envelopes sit on my bedside table, cards waiting to be opened tomorrow. One from Tess, one from Finn, with a small, hard bumpy shape inside that might be a bracelet. There's a jiffy bag with a London postmark and a Mars bar kind of feel to it, addressed for the first time in Mouse's own big, wobbly writing.

Nothing from Storm. Why am I surprised?

She wrote at Christmas, anyhow, so I guess I can't complain. She sent me a length of sari fabric, purple silk shot through with silver threads. I've hung it at my bedroom window, along with the flowery fairy lights that used to drape round the pinboard.

*Dizzy, babe,* she wrote,

*Hope you like the sari. Someone gave it to me, but it's silk, and vegans don't wear silk, so I thought of you. You'd love Goa, Dizz, I wish your Dad would loosen up a bit and let you come stay. We'd have the wildest time. Zak says hi. We're sitting on the beach, listening to rave music, just smoking and watching the stars above a silver sea. How cool is that?*

    *Love,*

        *Storm xxxxx*

It's cool, Storm, pretty cool. Maybe I will go, one day.

Maybe not.

I switch the light off, slip into bed.

The breeze rustles the purple silk, and beyond it I see the night sky, mottled orange from the city's streetlamp glow. If Storm looks up from her beach in Goa, she'll see the Pole Star, hanging there in the velvet dark. If Finn looks out of his window in Lancashire, he'll see it, too. Mouse, in London, won't even be looking.

I'm looking, though. All I see is the orange glow, the soft, bruised shimmer of city sky. I can't see the Pole Star, but I can feel it, dream it.

I know it's there.

# Follow your dreams with all
# cathy cassidy's
# gorgeous books

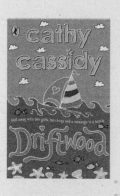

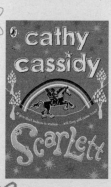

A real adventure. A true friend. Meet …

# Indigo Blue

Across the table, Anisha Patel is giving me a long, sad-eyed look too, which is the last thing I need. I can just imagine their faces if I tell them what's really going on. Even the edited highlights don't bear thinking about. On the other hand, it's not the kind of thing you can hide for long.

'I think we're moving house,' I say.

There's a silence. Anisha's eyes go all huge and anxious. Jo, by contrast, is frowning.

'Moving?' Jo says. 'You can't be. You've only been there a couple of years. It's dead nice, your house. Anyway, you can't be moving today, you've never even mentioned it before.'

'It was sort of a last-minute decision.'

'Fine,' says Jo. 'Suit yourself.'

Anisha makes an attempt to lighten the mood. 'Where are you moving to?'

How do you answer that one?

'I don't know,' I admit at last.

*Indie's life is falling apart – and she can't tell anybody. Not even her best friend, Jo. A yucky, smelly new flat is just the start of it. But there's a whole lot more to come . . .*

Out now!

# Hiya . . .

One of the coolest things about being a published author is getting the chance to meet my readers! Forget the flash car, the only thing I really wanted to buy with my advance was a VW camper van! It's fab to take it to bookshops, libraries, schools and festivals, and that's how the Cathy Cassidy Friendship Festival evolved. A friendship festival is all about having fun – and making new friends! There's always plenty to do – quizzes, hair-braiding, friendship bracelets, face-painting . . . and music and munchies, of course!

Friendship is something worth celebrating, so why not use these ideas to put on your own Friendship Festival . . . go for it!

*Cathy Cassidy*
x

## Getting ready:

- Send all your friends an invitation telling them where and when the Friendship Festival is happening

- You could ask everyone to dress up for the event and maybe award a prize for the best outfit

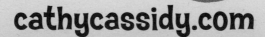

## cathycassidy.com

## On the day:

- Set the scene by decorating the venue with brightly coloured streamers and balloons

- Announce the start of the Friendship Festival and explain how Cathy tours the country with her van

- Gather everyone together and read a chapter from one of Cathy's books

- Friendship bracelets are great fun to make. All you need to do is buy some brightly coloured thread and then plait three strings together. It's easier if you work in pairs and get a bit of adult help to start you off

- There are lots of other things you can do to make your Friendship Festival really special, such as hair-braiding, funky music, make-overs, hand-/face-painting, nail art, T-shirt customizing, drinks and munchies, competitions, sleepovers, henna tattoos and lots of other craft activities (e.g. making bookmarks out of thread and beads). Have fun!

# cathycassidy.com

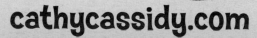

**BEST FRIENDS** are there for you in the good times and the bad. They can keep a secret and understand the healing power of chocolate.

**BEST FRIENDS** make you laugh and make you happy. They are there when things go wrong, and never expect any thanks.

**BEST FRIENDS** are forever,

# BEST FRIENDS ROCK!

cathy cassidy's
**My Best Friend Rocks!**
enter at
cathycassidy.com
mizz
award

**IS YOUR BEST FRIEND ONE IN A MILLION?**
Go to **cathycassidy.com**
to find out how you can show your
best friend how much you care